COLLISION THEORY

A NOVEL

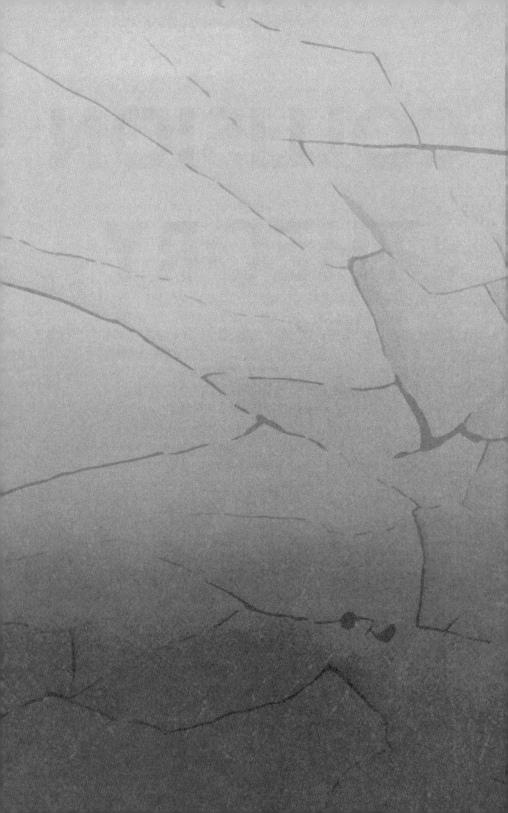

COLLISION THEORY

ADRIAN TODD ZUNIGA

A NOVEL

A BARNACLE BOOK | RARE BIRD BOOKS
LOS ANGELES, CALIF.

A Genuine Barnacle Book

A Barnacle Book | Rare Bird Books
453 South Spring Street, Suite 302
Los Angeles, CA 90013
rarebirdbooks.com

Set in Dante
Printed in the United States

10 9 8 7 6 5 4 3 2 1

Publisher's Cataloging-in-Publication data
Names: Zuniga, Adrian Todd, author.
Title: Collision theory : a novel / Adrian Todd Zuniga.
Description: First Trade Paperback Original Edition | A Genuine
Barnacle Book | New York, NY; Los Angeles, CA:
Rare Bird Books, 2018.
Identifiers: ISBN 9781945572821
Subjects: LCSH Family—Fiction. | Suicide—Fiction. | Psychological
fiction. | Humor fiction. | Literary fiction. | Black humor. | BISAC
FICTION / Literary | FICTION / Humorous / Black Humor
Classification: LCC PS3626 .U53 2018 | DDC 813.6—dc23

To my mother,
who loved when I was at home reading
because it meant I was near her,
which meant I was safe.

ONE

FIRST, I NOTICE HER standing on the building's ledge in low-slung sunlight, looking out over the city. Next, I spy her bare feet.

It's the way her shoes are settled at the base of the ledge—high heels kicked over, ankle straps still buckled—that tells me everything.

I'd come to the rooftop to breathe, but now there she is, seventy-five feet away. Beyond her, the Brooklyn Bridge held together by floss.

"I'll take you to dinner," I say, a prayer, as if my words could reverse gravity. But a whip of May wind catches my speech.

"We'll get far away from all of this right off," I shout. "Fly into Lisbon, then drive to Seville. We'll share a pitcher of sangria. You'll drink too much and I'll hold your hair back."

She continues to stare down the city's throat. I step toward her. The wind's hum lifts into a momentary whistle. The navy flowers on her dress rustle against her knees. She sways left to right in the C-sharp breeze.

"What's happened up until now," I shout louder, taking two steps, "I'll make it up to you times five."

The wind gusts and lolls. She reaches back to keep her dress down. Modesty, even now.

I take two more steps, but she's still so far away.

Her feet shift. She's seconds from takeoff.

"I'll ask you about your day and listen to every detail," I say. "We'll kiss under storm clouds until we're both soaked."

Her right foot inches to the ledge. Nothing I say anymore will matter.

"*Wait!*" I plead as I race toward her, then stop short.

She's rocking.

"Just *don't.*"

She's going to go.

"I know it's hard," I say. "I understand."

But I don't understand anything.

She turns and faces me. She raises her right hand and pulls a knotted strand of hair from her mouth and tucks it behind her right ear. Her cheeks are blotched red with upset, her mouth bent into an almost frown.

The wind tears across my eyes and the skyline blurs into watercolor. What I can half see is that she stops rocking. What I can half see are the birds pausing, the clouds braking. What I can see is that she has stopped *everything.*

Until.

Until she collapses like a faint and disappears from the ledge.

TWO

FIFTEEN MONTHS AFTER THE slow-motion encounter on my Brooklyn rooftop, my best friend calls.

"Thomas!" Ryan shouts to me through the phone. "Just a reminder that I arrive tomorrow into SFO at one."

Still in bed at 11:00 a.m., I sit up. "You what?"

"Did you not get my email?" he asks.

"I don't think so," I say. I can hear the cramp of London through the phone, flat sifts of rain and the sloshing zip of traffic. Outside my window, a brick wall is limned in bright, California sun.

"Fucking Vodaphone," he says. "One sec."

Ryan and I had been best friends since our freshman year at University of Missouri, though he'd been in the UK the last two years, writing for a TV show that hadn't made it stateside. We kept up on email and with texts, but the time change made it feel, most days, like he'd gone to the moon.

"Fuck!" he shouts into the phone. "It's still in my drafts folder. From a *month* ago. Shit! I'll send it now, but it basically asks if I can crash with you for a few days. But if it's a problem, I can…"

"Definitely stay with me," I say. "However long is fine."

"You're sure?" he asks. I can hear the smile in his voice. I don't know if he can hear the relief in mine.

"Positive," I say. "There's not a ton of space, but we'll make it work."

"The couch is fine."

"You'll have your own room," I say.

"Fancy," he says, like I'd hit it rich.

"Correction," I say, since I was little better than month to month. "You'll have your own *cubby-hole.*"

The space was the exact size of the slim, twin-sized fold-up cot I had in my apartment's lone closet.

"Awesome," he says. "Once I'm there, I'll take you out for the finest steak in town!"

"Great," I say with a laugh, the first in too long. He knew any sort of beef was an assault on my digestive system the way I knew he read the newspaper twice, annually. "Then I'll make sure my *New York Times* subscription is up to date."

❖ ❖ ❖

WHEN RYAN ARRIVES THE next afternoon, he says to me, "You gangly motherfucker!" then gives me a bear hug. He pulls back and says, "Seriously, gain some weight."

Which, after all these months of static life, I'm surprised I haven't.

"I guess I'll take yours?" I say, and point at his belly. "Clearly London's had an impact."

"It's all pies over there!" he says. "Pies and rain. I don't work out unless it's a cloudless day. You get my text?"

"Don't think so," I say, and pull out my phone to check. "Ah, there it is." When he sees I'm on a Motorola flip phone, he goes on the offensive.

"You don't seriously still use that thing?"

"This one's new," I say, proudly holding it up. "Sixteen bucks on eBay, and does everything I need."

"Except alert you to incoming texts from this century?" he says.

"You're right. I should probably upgrade to an iPhone that doesn't send emails."

"Fucker," he says.

I see he's only got two large bags with him. For an overseas move, I expected way more. "I thought you were leaving London for good?"

"I am," he says. "Pared it down to the essentials. This is all I've got left."

❖ ❖ ❖

ONCE RYAN'S INSIDE, HE sees the unpacked boxes, the stripped-down setup.

"Place is great," he says as we walk past my bedroom, which is just a bed, folded T-shirts and underwear atop never-opened boxes, and two paintings leaned against the wall. When we pass the living room—a TV, couch, and coffee table; nothing on the walls, not a plant in sight—Ryan asks, "You just move in?"

"A year ago," I say, embarrassed to see this place, now, through someone else's eyes. Any excitement of Ryan's visit edges quickly toward the dread of being exposed as a shut-in. So I try to cover. "Just kept it spartan in case…"

"In case of end times?" Ryan cracks, letting me off the hook, which allows me to relax. "I mean, why unpack just so the world can eventually, someday end once you've done all that work?"

At the rear of the apartment where Ryan will sleep, the bed's so tight to the walls on three sides the comforter is impossible to tuck in. I'd set a chair at the end of the bed, where we're now standing, to serve as an end table.

"Sorry," I say.

"For what? It's palatial!" he says. "There's more than enough room. And this will fit perfectly below." He slides one of his bulging bags beneath the mattress, and it does fit perfectly below. But when he tries to follow with the second, there's no way.

"I've got room in my closet."

My closet showcases a trio of basic suits for work: black, gray, navy; four white shirts; the bespoke blue-white wool blazer Sarah got me for my birthday two years ago; and boxes. Ryan's second bag fits in the space where, yesterday, the cot was. Once it's stowed, we plop onto the couch and he asks me, "What have you been up to? Besides, y'know, unpacking? Like, what's been going on? I feel like you've been stingy with details since you left New York."

"Still a paralegal," I say, with a smile intended to mask how directionless my work is. "I've been bouncing between a handful of firms doing contract work when they need me. Pays the rent."

"So you're loving every minute of it?" he says with a laugh and sits up. "You dating anyone?"

I let out a long sigh. He gives me a pitying, *Oh no* look.

"Yeah, I haven't tried at all since Sarah." I ask, "What about you?"

"But, wait," he starts.

"Sarah's gone," I tell him, eager to change the subject. "There's just nothing to say."

"Sorry. But I get it," he says. "As for me, I never told you about Delphine."

"Delphine?"

"Yeah," he says, and falls back. He stares at the ceiling. "I never talked about her, because—this is so dumb—but I didn't want to *jinx* it. But in the end, it wasn't up to me. Three months after our first date, she got a job offer in Vienna. I was in bed next to her when she got the call, and she didn't hesitate. Accepted right away." He punches out a sigh. "God, that sucked."

"Sorry," I say.

"I told her I'd go with her," he says. "That I'd move to Vienna." He covers his face with his hands, embarrassed.

"What'd she say?"

"She laughed! She said, 'Verry fun*n*y,'" Ryan says, mirroring Delphine's French accent. "So I laughed, too, and told her I'd miss her."

"What'd she say to that?"

"Her exact words: 'Zometimes I miz you, too. But this wuz, uhh, not so zarious, ouais?'" Ryan sits up. "And the hard part? While I was thinking she may be my future wife, it wasn't serious for her, at all. She left a month later. And even though my writing gig with Channel Four was done, I stuck around London, spent my days writing this new TV pilot, all with my fingers crossed that she'd call to say...*anything*. But she never called. Just sent one email to say how busy the new job was keeping her, and to see if she'd left a pair of gold earrings on my nightstand."

"Oof," I say. "That sucks. But if it's any consolation, I'm glad you're here."

"Here's to us in SF," Ryan says, raising his fist. I bump it with my own. "Honored guests in the Home for Wayward Hearts."

THREE

FOUR MONTHS LATER, RYAN tells me he's too sick to get out of bed. He's been projectile vomiting all night.

It's 6:00 a.m. on pitch day, and we're supposed to leave for the airport in half an hour.

"We have to cancel," he croaks.

"We can't cancel." I tell him how low I'm running on funds, that we booked nonrefundable flights, plus the car rental and hotel were prepaid.

"But if we blow this..."

"I won't blow it," I say, an unconvincing blurt. Though, I'd largely leaned on Ryan to lead the pitch. Had only done two full run-throughs on my own, both so he could monitor how it sounded in someone else's voice.

"Okay," he says.

"Okay?" Now, suddenly ripped with panic after an anxious sleep, I want him to overrule me. "You're sure?"

"No," he says with a weak laugh. "But these sorts of things? You just never know."

"Maybe I shouldn't go." I stood there, giving him one last chance to let me off the hook.

"You should," he says. "You're right. You got this."

❖❖❖

WHAT RYAN THINKS I'VE got is our *Attack On Graceland* movie pitch. Born from me bailing on contract work week after week, and him taking a break after submitting his latest TV pilot to his agent, we'd spend our afternoons and evenings binge-watching the tacky, harebrained entirety of Elvis Presley's thirty-one film catalogue. Our movie concept was triggered by post-viewing, deep-dive conversations about The King. Would any of these films be made today? Was he a sneaky-good actor? What would a Tarantino-directed Elvis film look like? Or Charlie Kaufman? What if Graceland were a terrorist target?

"What if aliens came to earth to steal it?" I asked at one point.

Ryan leaned forward and stared at me.

I wiped at my face, wondering if there was something on it. "What?"

He pointed at me. "We should write that."

"Write what?"

"What you just said—the alien thing."

Which led to the two of us spending our mornings at a nearby café brainstorming a series of wild plot points and weirdo characters, then slowly crystallizing them into an absurd, feature-length movie concept about aliens poaching Elvis's Graceland.

"We could sell this," Ryan had said.

"How? It's so dumb." Still, a glimmer of possibility fizzed in my head.

Weeks later, Ryan came into my room and surprised me when he told me that three production companies—all in LA, all with the money to green-light films—said they'd be willing to hear our Elvis-based movie pitch.

❖❖❖

SO, AFTER MY FOG-DELAYED flight from SFO to LAX, followed by a rental car sprint to drop my luggage at the Best Western Plus above the 101 Café on Franklin—contemporary lodging with a retro vibe!—I motor toward West Hollywood, and after a creeping crawl of traffic on Sunset, I can't believe my luck when I find metered parking across the street from the first pitch meeting. With no idea how long the pitch will take, I go all in and fill the meter for two hours' worth. As I hustle to the intersection, it hits me that I will, very shortly, try—*all alone; oh, god what have I done!*—to convince powerful people that Ryan and I have created a story that is an all-around can't-miss.

I time the stoplight just right, shoot across the street, and once I enter the lobby of the building, I pull out my phone to see that I am not on time—the car's GPS lied!—when I bump into someone or someone bumps into me. My phone hurtles floor-ward and clatters into two on contact: the battery and the *phone* part of the phone.

A woman with curly brown hair pulled back and tired eyes spins around, reads the look on my face. "I'm so sorry," she says.

"It's fine," I say, frantic as I search the floor for the pieces amongst furniture and potted plants. I see the battery, which she snatches up first and holds it out to me with a straight arm.

"Don't worry, we're going to find—is it your camera?"

I tell her it's my phone.

"Oh, god. Your *phone?*"

"It's ancient," I say, as way of explaining why there are two pieces. "It's like...a flip phone."

She doesn't judge, instead she does what I'm doing: scans the ground for the phone part of the phone—the important part.

"I'm such a klutz," she says.

"No, it's fine. I'm just late for a *really* important meeting. Fuck! Where'd it *go*?"

"I'll *fix* this," she says. Her eyes light with newfound commitment. "Go. I'll find your phone and get it back to you. I don't live too far. You shouldn't be late."

"You're sure?"

"It's the least I can do," she says. "But I'll need that." She points at the battery. I hand it over without a thought.

I slow walk toward the elevator in a daze of uncertainty.

"Oh, what's your number?" she asks from behind me.

I point at the black battery in her palm. "*That's* my phone number."

"Oh, duh. Jeez. Okay, so call when you're done," she says. I nod, dumbfounded, obviously not understanding. "You call *your* number," she says patiently. "I'll answer *your* phone and get it back to you."

I don't get it, but there's no time to think it through as I back toward the elevator. Then I get it. "Oh!" I say. "I'll call *you* on *my* phone. Yes, got it. Thank you!"

The elevator bell dings, which spurs me to turn without another thought. I hop inside, then right as the doors close, it hits me: *Wouldn't it be easier for her to leave my phone with reception?*

"Wait!" I call out to her as I turn.

But the doors are closed.

FOUR

Alone in an elevator that shoots me up to the fifteenth floor, I reach into my pocket to check the time on my phone, then panic—*Oh, fuck! It's gone!*—before remembering, duh, it's in the purse of a total stranger or being swept from dustpan to trashcan by a steadfast janitor.

I step to the side and use the mirrored frame around the elevator's doors to check in: my white shirt's maintained none of the crispness from last night's ironing and is trying hard to untuck from my jeans. I shove it back in, grab the lapels of my blue-white blazer to square the shoulders, then a quick check of my hair—a chestnut pompadour without the slick, highlighted by a thin streak of gray, just right of center. I tap the heels of my dull, black oxfords against the elevator floor, then do a close check of my eyes. They're dark from so little sleep, tinged with bloodshot.

Out of the elevator, I enter into the indistinct lobby of CollabCorp Productions, where I'm met by a wide-shouldered, midthirties man with a crew cut who's wearing a buttoned, pin-striped blue suit. "You must be Ryan."

Which immediately throws me.

"Oh, I'm Thomas, actually."

"And Ryan?" he asks.

"They didn't call to let you know?"

"Who didn't?"

"Peter, I guess? Our agent. Sorry. I thought they'd let you know Ryan's unwell and can't make it." I follow this with a pained apologetic expression. It's clear now, I was dumb to come alone. I am so totally unqualified for this.

"Hmm," he says as two lines on his forehead deepen and darken, then he shakes my hand. "Well, thank you for coming." He doesn't introduce himself. It's such a weird vibe, and I'm so rattled I don't ask his name.

He leads me into a plain, beige room with a group of four men and two women sitting in black leather chairs along one side of a conference room table. They all stand when I enter, and the taller of the two women says, "We were led to believe there'd be two of you?"

Fuck me.

I'm about to speak when the man who had led me into the room says, "The screenwriter couldn't make it. So it'll be just the one."

"The cocreator," I say, trying to bolster my reputation. But in this world, I have no reputation. Which seems obvious to everyone. "I'm Thomas."

"Not Ryan, then?" the woman says.

"No," I say. Then a beat before I stupidly repeat my name.

The woman processes this information with disappointment that surpasses that of the man who led me here.

"But I'm pretty fun," I say, to lighten the moment, which falls all-the-way flat.

"Please sit," she says with a forced smile.

I sit and expect a round of hellos but it's just silence.

"Go on," she says.

"You mean…" I say, unsure.

"We're ready."

"Right. Well, hello everyone," I say with a raise of my hand and a bow of my head. The response is light nods or nothing. Then silence. "So, I just start?"

"Please," the other woman says, like she's already lost her patience.

"So, the idea —"

"So, it's *just* in idea form?" one of the men asks.

"Excuse me?" I ask.

"There's no script?"

"Not yet, no. Just the outline and treatment. If you've had a chance to read those."

The man nods vaguely, which I take to mean three things: 1. he's not read a word; 2. it was a rookie mistake to bring it up at all; 3. I should get on with it.

"The idea is there's a guy named Lucas Ramsdell, a thirty-three-year-old bummer of a guy..."

"Is his being thirty-three imperative?" one of the men asks.

"Maybe he could be younger?" another of the men suggests.

"Well, maybe," I say. "But the thing is, he's a divorced mechanic who doesn't pay child support for his two sons. So, I'm not sure..."

"What else?" the tall woman asks.

"Well, okay, so he finds himself in Memphis where he gets on a tour bus to Graceland."

"Graceland," the second woman says, like she's maybe heard of it.

"Where Elvis lived," I say, then scan the stoic faces of The Zombified Six.

"Elvis," one of the men says. "The singer."

"Yeah," I say, and give it a second. "I hope I'm making some sort of sense."

The second woman says, "Does it make sense? I believe so." She looks around the room. Everyone nods. "I, for one, appreciate your coming here."

She looks around and confirms, with nods, that my coming was, in fact, worth appreciating.

I wait for quiet, then start up again, tell them, "And once inside the gates to Graceland, that's when…"

"Actually," the tall woman says, "I think we've got what we need on this for now."

"Okay, because that's basically just…"

"We can let your agent know about our final decision. As you've mentioned, we have the outline and the treatment for reference."

"Oh, great, so you have read the treatment." A quick scan of their faces and I see the only appropriate response would be to face-palm myself.

"Yes, we have," she says, very curt. "And I will say, it sounds very exciting."

"Absolutely," says one of the men. "It's a great, great idea."

"I love it," says another of the men.

I am so confused.

The tall woman stands, then they all do.

"Okay," I say, standing, too. "Thanks for seeing me?"

"Thank *you*," the tall one says.

No one makes a move to shake my hand, so I bow a goodbye and back out the door, where I'm intercepted by the guy in the pin-striped blue suit.

"This way," he says, and holds out his arm as a guide. I walk ahead of him, taking long, purposeful strides. When he says thanks for coming, I hurry out of CollabCorp's front door with a wave and rush into the indistinct, fifteenth-floor lobby. When I find the elevator doors are open, I race inside, so thoroughly grateful that I don't have to spend another second there. It's a bonus that the elevator happens to be going down.

When the doors close, a swarm of stinging wasps bursts loose inside my chest. I hate that I don't have my phone, because I have no way to call Ryan to apologize for all my micro-fuckups that led to the brutal boot out the CollabCorp door.

When the elevator hits the ground floor, I head to the exit with my head on a swivel, in case the stranger who promised to return my phone might still be local. But no luck.

I push through the door into the whoosh and hum of the city, where I take a deep, rattled breath. By the time I'm back at my rental car, my initial desire to apologize to Ryan has been replaced by anger. I'm desperate to ask him what the fuck just happened. When I see there's an hour and forty-nine minutes still on my meter, I can't stop myself from loosing a cleansing "Fuck *that*." I get in the car and glance at the building I just came from. A shudder runs through me, like my soul is trying to shake off the last nine minutes of my life. But at the same time, I feel a weird sort of freedom, like I've escaped.

FIVE

With all kinds of time still left on my parking meter, I decide not to pull away just yet, and instead do a thing I haven't done in over a decade: hunt for a payphone. I'm stunned to find one a block and a half away from me, and wonder how many payphones I've passed by over the last ten years that never even registered. How many things I see daily that I pass without any recognition. How I should pay closer attention to the details.

I lift the payphone receiver and insert my credit card into the slot, so I can dial into my voicemail. The digitized voice of a woman I'll never meet says: "*Two* new messages."

The first message is from Ryan, who asks, "Who's the girl that just answered your phone? That's fucked up. You okay? I wanted to wish you luck with CollabCorp, but instead this suspicious girl answers? So I'm a little freaked out. Ryan update: I've had to run to the toilet six hundred times since you left. Call me when you're out. Bye."

The second is Ryan, again. "I just made that strange-o chick promise she hasn't killed you. Has she? I hope you're alive and I hope the pitch is going okay and that you can feel my support from head top to ham hock. Okay, I've gotta go throw up or worse. Call me back!"

Relieved my phone is in working order, I stick my credit card back into the payphone slot and dial Ryan.

"You haven't been murdered!" he says when he answers.

"Close enough. The assholes at that pitch meeting—holy fuck, dude. That was the most soul-harming three minutes of my life."

"Shit," Ryan says, and I hear the air go out of him. Which ramps up my feeling of letting him down. "Only three minutes? So they hated it?"

"It was weirder than that. Honestly, I'm not sure they'd ever heard of Elvis. Maybe I use his last name next time."

I hear Ryan breathing. "They didn't like the Vaseline cathedral line?"

"Didn't get to it."

"Oh. Well, how'd they respond to the Pat Boone line?"

"I didn't get that far."

Another pause. More breathing.

"But it's right at the start," Ryan says.

"I'm telling you, it was super weird."

"Okay, of course. Yeah. I'm just...fuck."

It feels horrid, standing at this payphone, feeling like I blew it, being judged, being here all alone.

"People can be real dicks," he says. "But it's okay."

"Is it? I mean, is it all going to be like this?"

"I hope not. I guess it's like anything, you're not always going to vibe with people."

"Forget vibing—what about just, like, human decency?"

"I know," Ryan says, energyless. "I'm surprised Peter would think they'd be into it if they were that far not into it."

"I think they just weren't into *me*. If you'd been here..."

"Nah. I'm not star power," Ryan says. "They don't know my face. You could say you're me in a pinch, and it'd all be the same. But if you want to bail on the last two and hold off until we can do this together, I mean, I get it."

"No," I say, as a bolt of ego rises up in me. "I'm here, the meetings are set. I'll do the next, then reassess."

"Alright," he says, and any discouragement fades from his voice. "Sounds like you're warmed up!"

"I'd say overheated. I really want bad things to happen to those CollabCorp automatons."

"I like the passion!" Ryan says. "And the best way to stick it to them is nail the next meeting. Then they'll wish they'd listened. My stomach's cartwheeling, so I gotta go in a sec. But what's up with your phone? And who's that girl?"

I tell him what happened.

"So you let her *keep* your phone?"

"I panicked because I was running late."

"All right," Ryan says with a laugh. "Uh-oh. Bathroom's calling. Gotta go! Ring me after the next pitch. Or when you get your phone back. *Oh, god!*"

SIX

I DIAL MY CELL phone number. It takes two rings before the voice of the woman who promised to find my phone answers with, "Yes, hello?" Her voice is anxious and eager.

"It's Thomas," I say. "The one who bumped into you. I own the phone?"

"I know who you are," she says. "Look, people have been calling asking for you. Your dad called and told me about your mom. He thought I was Sarah?"

"Oh, no," I say. But it's my fault for telling my parents, during our weekly calls over the last year-plus, that I'm okay, that I'm doing well, in fact, that Sarah's taking good care of me.

"Y'know what, can we just meet, please? So I can give you your phone back?"

It takes me a second to tell her, "Sure. Tell me where."

"I'm at six-one-two-one Glen Tower Road," she says.

I repeat the address.

"Hurry, please," she says. Then something else, but her voice dies out from a crackle of static, a rain cloud sucking up her voice.

"Hello?" I say. "You there?"

But she's gone. I still don't know her name.

SEVEN

I DRIVE NORTH ON Beachwood Drive in a hurry, past palm trees, squat and lean, that hide a mix of low homes and styleless two-story apartment buildings. I lean forward to see the Hollywood sign laid out bright and high in the distance before I turn left onto a skimp of a street. I park in a cramped space between two compacts, then I find 6121 and the mailbox for E. Morris. Her place is the adult equivalent of a tree house positioned high on a hill.

I feel myself withdraw as I climb up-up-up a bending wooden staircase grooved into a lush hill scattered with weak-stemmed flowers. My hope is we'll race through pleasantries, I'll get my phone, and go. But that seems less likely once I'm on her worn, petrified deck. E. Morris comes out of her front door and onto her deck, talking to someone on my phone, laughing.

It gives me a moment to take my first good look at E. Morris. She's dressed down, now, out of the business attire I saw her in less than an hour ago, and her paint-stained sleeveless T-shirt shows off too-thin arms. Her hair is a curly confusion of brown streaked with blonde. My guess is she's no older than thirty-three, which is my age.

"Uh-huh," E. says into my phone. She mouths a *hi!* to me, mouths *it's your mother!* "He's right here. Yes, right here. Yep, he made it. Of course you can talk to him!"

E. offers me my phone. Her smile is filled with hopeful possibilities. But the thought of talking to my unwell mother with a witness present makes me feel faint. I lean back to keep balance.

"She's in good spirits," E. tells me.

I take a deep breath, then take my phone. "Hello?" I say. My skin heats then cools.

"She's very sweet," my mother says, her voice sounding weak, staggered with phlegm.

I flash a glance at E. "I guess," I say, a strain.

Mom coughs like a grumble and my eyes go wet. She asks me, "Are you okay?"

"I think so." I put my free hand over my forehead, to cover my eyes, in case.

"We need to talk," Mom says.

"Okay."

"Not on the phone," she says. "I'd really like if you could please come home."

"*Mom*," I say, and my voice cracks. "You know I can't."

"Oh, Thomas," she says, an appeal in her voice that's able to mask any exasperation. "It's been nearly two years."

Twenty-two months. But I don't correct her. Instead, I take my hand from my face and close my eyes while inhaling a long, slow breath. Then I hang up.

E. looks at me, shocked. "Did you just hang up on her?"

I can't look her in the eye.

"She needs you."

I feel a quick flare of anger rise inside me. "You don't know anything about it."

But E. doesn't back down. "I know she's sick. I know Ryan keeps throwing up, and that you're in LA to pitch a movie. So I know something."

"Thanks for getting my phone back," I say, and slip it into my front pocket. Then I turn and head toward the stairs.

"I'm sorry," E. says, following me. "But can you at least tell me who Sarah is?"

I stop, shake my head.

"Can I guess?"

I don't react.

"Is she your girlfriend?"

I let out a swift exhale, then continue across the creaking deck toward the stairs.

"Your wife?"

"No."

"Who then?"

"She's no one."

"Well, she *must* be someone if that's who your mother thought I was."

I'm at the stairs when I register something in her tone that makes me turn. When our eyes meet, hers are full of apology. "I didn't *mean* to."

"You didn't *mean* to?" I laugh, baffled by the intrusiveness of E.'s action. "Holy fucking shit." I start down the stairs, away from this crazy.

"Please don't go yet," E. pleads.

I'm glad she stops me, so I can ask one last question: "Why did you even answer when my mother called?"

"I thought it was you! Calling to get your phone back."

Which is fair. But. "And when it wasn't, first chance you got, you said you were Sarah."

"I'm sorry!" says E. "Her voice was so brittle. Before I knew it, I'd said it. Then I felt like I couldn't take it back."

"Why not?"

"I know this'll sound nuts, but I didn't want to be a liar."

I can't get away fast enough, but as I pound down the stairs, E. follows. "And then your father called. Then your mom, again…"

My phone vibrates in my pocket. I slow so I can pop it open. A text from Ryan asks: "Did Thomas steal his phone back, yet? Though I guess I should just text you to ask that?"

I hear the ding of E.'s phone behind me—a result of Ryan's copy and paste.

"Can you wait a second, please?" E. asks me.

I hurry to the bottom of the stairs.

"I want to make it up to you. I can make you something to eat, then we'll call your mom and I'll tell her the truth."

Her plea to set the record straight jostles something free in my brain, and it occurs to me that what E.'s done could be a positive. If Mom's health spirals, she'll continue to believe I'm not alone, that Sarah isn't just rumor.

"Or I can just call her," she says.

I stop so fast I nearly trip. "Don't," I say, afraid she might anyway. So I give her a hard stare. "What you've done, stays done."

"Okay," she says, as I reach my rental car. "Okay."

I check the time before I get in. *Shit.* The next pitch meeting is in twenty-five minutes. And I'm at least twenty minutes away.

"*Fuck*," I say.

"What?" she asks behind me, arms crossed, a guarded position.

"*Ask Ryan,*" I say, a show of contempt for her clear and obvious trespass.

EIGHT

O N MY WAY TO my second meeting, after I take my third wrong turn, a check of the clock makes it official: I'm late. As I stuff my car into a tight space on a nearby side street, the car's air-conditioning loses out to my stress. Salty blossoms open on my forehead and beads of tickling sweat run down my back. I exit the car feeling wet.

❖❖❖

I HUSTLE INTO A bland lobby, race up two flights of concrete stairs, then pass through the glass doors to Anarchy Productions. The entrance is bright, a wood-floored office with battered leather couches pressed against white walls that are lined with posters of movies they've made. Movies I've seen, and liked. Or think I've seen. At least heard of?

"Can I help you?" The receptionist for Anarchy is a blot of color that sits at an all-white desk, against a backdrop of exposed brick. Lime-colored, rectangular glasses are perched on her nose. Her mauve-colored collar spreads over the lapels of a gray wool jacket. Behind her is Anarchy's logo: an ironically neat "A" cased in black, interrupted by a wild, spray-painted yellow slash, which holds the word "Films."

"I'm Thomas," I say, out of breath, mouth dry.

"Thomas?"

"I have a one thirty appointment with Sam Gerrard and Figgy Becht." The way I pronounce Becht is *Besht*.

"And your *last* name?" she asks, maybe annoyed.

"Oh, sorry. Mullen."

She looks into her schedule book. "And Ryan Ahearn," she says as she checks something off.

Fuck. I should have called. Or Ryan? Though, really, wasn't that Peter's job?

"He's not feeling well," I say. But the unrehearsed tone of my excuse sounds pale, like Ryan *didn't feel like it*.

"They're running a bit late, if you'd like to have a seat."

Relieved that I'll have a chance to refresh, I ask, "Is there a restroom close?"

She points at the door I came through. "On the left." As I turn to go she tells me, "And it's pronounced Be*k*t."

"Oh," I say, and an all-new heat hits my body.

❖❖❖

IN THE BATHROOM, I'M anxious they'll be ready to meet before I'm back, so I hurry things along: flush while I'm still urinating, button my fly one-handed while blowing my nose into a wad of toilet paper, and fix my hair while I wash my free hand.

I hustle back into Anarchy's office, but a light nod from the receptionist tells me the only urgency is mine. I sit, sink deep into one of the leather couches and fiddle with the button on my jacket sleeve, and try to relax. I mentally prep by telling myself that if they're willing to listen, I'm going to nail this. I *have* to nail this. For one, I have to counter Ryan's rising doubt that I should have come at all. And two, for the last three months, I've turned down every single opportunity for contract work. After I pay off rent and expenses in two weeks, I'll be on fiscal fumes. And all this with the added stress of Mom and Dad pushing to get me home.

But for all my concerns, if these people are dicks like CollabCorp, then fuck them. What Ryan and I created? It's good. I'm proud of it. So I'm not going to let them shit on it. And if they act blasé, then maybe I stand and tell them, *Thanks, but we're going to go another direction.* Because what's the harm? We alienate a production company that wants nothing to do with us?

So I'll do my part. I'll start as clean as I can at the top, then pitch them fast to get to the good stuff. I'll give them every reason to believe. And if they don't like it or it's not for them, fine. But if they're disrespectful? Two can play at that game.

So now I'm mad. In hyperdrive. Agitated and spinning. To get myself back on a calmer track, I use an age-old trick my mother taught me: ask a stranger a question.

"Do you like Elvis?" I ask the receptionist.

She looks up, surprised. "Presley, Costello, or Mitchell?"

"*Mitchell?*"

"The film critic. He's very good."

"I mean The King," I say in a way that indicates the other two don't count.

"I like when he wiggles."

I laugh and look down, calmer now. The receptionist goes back to whatever's on her iMac screen, and I spend the next minutes trying to position myself so I come off as somewhat cool when Sam and Figgy come out to get me. I sit with my hands crossed on my lap, then uncross my legs and study my palms. I keep adjusting, but only slightly, so the receptionist won't notice. I glance over to see if she's noticed, but now she's head-down, silently reading a magazine. So I watch the clock.

Then in walks a guy my age. Which means...*shit.* They're hearing other pitches! Which, of course they are. But I don't want to know that. My breath goes short, my heart bangs hard in my chest. An anxiety spiral that makes me tell myself: *No, no, no. You're fine, you're fine, you're fine.*

He's wide-shouldered with a confident gait, and when he's midway to the receptionist he says his full name—Nicholas Leary—scoring what I perceive to be instant points. He says he's here for a pitch meeting with Sam Gerrard and Figgy Becht (he correctly pronounces Becht as *Bekt*), and says he's sorry he's so early. She tells him it's no problem, but they are running a little behind if he wants to come back in half an hour.

"Happy to wait, if that's all right," he says confidently. She smiles up at him in a way that she didn't smile up at me—the same way I bet she'd have smiled at Ryan because he has an IMDB page. Then Nicholas sits on the couch across from me and says, "Hey."

I nod. Knowing I've lost.

That I don't belong here without Ryan.

That our idea is a joke that's progressed too far.

That after being alone for too long, I let the euphoria of collaboration outweigh the common sense of real work.

I should go. Claim a flu bug. Fake-receive a call and say it's an emergency. Just get up and leave.

I open my mouth to tell the receptionist, "Excuse me…" but don't get past the open-mouthed bark of the E. when her desk buzzer sounds. "Mimi?" a voice asks.

Mimi picks up her phone. "Yes?" A beat. "I sure can."

Mimi sets down the phone and lifts off of her seat.

"Thomas?"

"Yes?" I ask, surprised.

"You can go on in. Second door on the left."

"Cool," I say in a way that's most definitely uncool. Then I give Nicholas a look of, *Here we go.*

"Good luck," he says.

Which throws me. Because isn't this competition? Aren't we head-to-head? Though, maybe not. Not exactly. Anarchy makes ten films a year. Everyone into the pool, right?

I get up slow and remind myself to be defiant in the face of even mild contempt, to be fierce.

As I make my way in, Nicholas says with confident cheer, "Mimi? Really? That's my mother's name."

I pause at Mimi's desk.

"My mom's name is Rosemary," I tell her quietly.

"Oh," Mimi says, looking at me, surprised.

"Huh," Nicholas says behind me. "Cool."

I turn and look at him, then back at Mimi. An awkward moment I let last too long before I nod and head in, heart once again racing, toward the second door on the left.

NINE

THE SECOND DOOR ON the left leads me into a room with decoration-free exposed brick walls, and along those walls there are stacks of different movie posters that come hip high, and a mound of tote bags with the Anarchy brand mark. Figgy and Sam, the British minds behind Anarchy, sit in high-backed chairs behind a wide, nicked-to-shit wooden table made of a dozen battered-then-glazed 4x4s. Behind them, high, arching windows see across to another building with smaller, less-arching windows.

"Thomas!" Sam and Figgy say in unison when I walk in, raising their hands as a welcome. Their reaction and their age—they're both in their late thirties—relax me immediately.

"Hey, guys, thanks so much for taking the time to meet. Ryan's not feeling well, so..."

"No wukking furries, mate—Mimi sent a note on," Figgy says in a soft British accent I can easily understand.

I walk toward the table and they both rise to shake my hand. I shake Figgy's first; underneath his right eye is a scar the length of my pinky. Then I shake Sam's—catching half a handful of sleeve from his oversized, clover-green sweat suit top that says C E L T I C.

"Have a seat, mate," Figgy says, so I do.

I sit, and I'm about to start when I see Figgy's pressing his lips together so hard they've gone white and Sam's face warps into a forced frown. Before I can ask what's going on, Figgy bursts out laughing, then Sam follows suit—a dangle of white spittle attaches to the shaggy clumps of facial hair that make up his beard. These two men are seriously losing their shit, their pale complexions both bright red with laughter, and since I don't get the joke, I do the only thing I can and offer a wide-eyed look of pleasantness and a forced smile to show what a great sport I am.

Figgy sees I'm lost and holds up his hand as an apology, then pulls his T-shirt over his nose and mouth.

"Sorry, mate. Sorry," Sam says. His rich accent and hurried, open-mouthed delivery borders on cockney.

The joke is still lost on me.

Then it hits me: *the smell*. I wince. Figgy and Sam see my reaction and belt out whoops of new laughter. Figgy pulls his T-shirt away from his face and coughs into his hand.

"This one's got a bit of an exploding bum," Figgy says.

"That's my last go with soyrizo."

I nod, relieved to know what all the laughter's about. I put my hand over my face and pinch my nose to show that I am now, officially, in on the joke.

"Now that's outta the way…" Figgy says, and folds his hands.

Sam wipes his mouth with the back of his sleeve, disintegrating the string of spittle. "All right. Let's have it, then," Figgy says, and their faces take on an immediate, serious look. "Whatcha got?"

I zip through the start of my pitch so quick that Sam interrupts me midsentence. "I ain't mutton, but you're nearly fucking inaudible," he says.

"He's all in a rush for fear you'll deliver another trouser trumpet," Figgy says.

"Fair play," Sam says. "You start over and slow down and I promise to keep a clamp on my colon." He pronounces it co-*LON*.

Figgy and Sam smile at me. I nod and smile back.

"Okay," I say, realizing I've overreacted to the odd hell of the CollabCorp pitch. "Sorry about that."

"*Right*. Now, tell us what your movie's about."

Heart racing, I start over. I tell them as clear and calm as I can, "Lucas Ramsdell is a thirty-three-year-old divorced mechanic who doesn't pay child support for his daughter."

Figgy's eyebrows raise, a momentary frown. "Real stand-up geezer," Figgy jokes.

"Exactly," I say, and his immediate feedback relaxes me. My heart slows. I sit up straighter. "So, after drifting to Memphis, Lucas does his usual dismissing of his life's core responsibilities and hops a tour bus to Graceland, Elvis Presley's modern-day mansion."

Figgy leans forward. I take it as an encouraging sign.

"The gates to Graceland open, the tour bus goes through, and right when the gates close—bang! *Martians swarm the bus.* They're classic-issue aliens—big teardrop-shaped eyes, huge foreheads, tiny Japanimation mouths—except for one major twist: they're all dressed as Elvis impersonators. Jet black, pomaded pompadours like Vaseline cathedrals. Bushy sideburns. They're wearing satin jumpsuits, jackets with upturned collars, and fluffs of chest hair. It's clear, based on the way they're dressed, that Elvis is their religion."

"Nice one," Sam says, scratching at his beard as he leans way back in his chair.

"Lucas sneaks from the back of the bus, ditching everyone else, and makes a run for it. He races to an ivy-covered wall that's low enough for him to climb over when *poof!* Elvis's ghost appears. The King himself, drawn in stardust. He tells Lucas…" here I dip into my best Elvis-speak, one meager skill

I have over Ryan—"'You can't go nowhere, *mahn*. Come on. *Mahn*, ya gotta save Graceland.'"

Figgy claps and laughs. He looks over at Sam who's all smiles.

"Can't go nowhere, *mahn*," Sam parrots in a brutal Elvis impersonation that makes him sound like a high-pitched Texan.

Delighted by the shoddy effort, Figgy gives it a go with a version of Elvis that sounds like he never got west of Leeds, let alone near Memphis. "Yuh gotta save Gracelan'."

They both clap and laugh.

"Fucking contagious that," Sam says, leaning forward, his forearms on the table now. Then gestures for me to go on.

I'm smiling. This is *fun*. And because of that, I enter a sort of flow.

"Lucas tells him, 'Screw you, Elvis, I'm a Pat Boone man!' and there's no way he's risking mutilation by alien Elvis's to save a mansion he doesn't give two diddles about. So Ghost Elvis gets real. He says, 'Lucas, ya been wastin' yer days, *mahn*. Now, I ain't sayin' it's the influence of Pat Boone's lesser euphonics, but yer whole life's been one big fat joke. You ain't nothin' but a nobody refusin' his destiny. This is yer one chance to mean sumthin'."

I look at Figgy then Sam. "This still making sense?"

"Marvelously," Figgy says.

Marvelously!

"Thank god," I say with a laugh, and let loose a sharp exhale before I go on. "Now, because Elvis distracted Lucas from hightailing it over the wall, a crew of *Jailhouse Rock* extraterrestrials are right on his heels. He can't make it over the wall in time, but he sees a clear path to Graceland. So he hauls ass toward the mansion to save himself, which means it's now Lucas Ramsdell, reluctant antihero, against a band of Elvis-impersonating aliens."

Sam and Figgy look at one another with crossed arms and nod.

"Lucas stays alive by defending himself with Elvis memorabilia from those awful-but-lovable movies. He uses boxing gloves from *Kid Galahad* as his first line of defense, then an oar from *Fun in Acapulco* to beat the aliens back. At one point he gets overrun, with only the ukulele from Blue Hawaii to defend himself. That's when the spirit of Elvis enters into Lucas's body so he can play *Can't Help Falling in Love,* which hypnotizes the aliens, allowing Lucas to get away."

I pause to gauge interest. Figgy gestures with his index finger, a rolling motion, to go on. So I go on.

"While Lucas awaits rescue, he discovers two things. One, the aliens hijacked the bus for hostages, meaning the Memphis PD and the military can't easily intervene. And two is the biggie. After enlisting the help of another escapee—a girl from the tour bus who can't *stand* him; and she accounts for the love interest/B story—Lucas learns that the aliens are building a huge rocket onto the side of the mansion with the intention of kidnapping Graceland right off the face of the earth. It's a race against the clock and if Lucas loses, the rocket will take off with Graceland in tow—along with all of the other captives, Lucas included, inside of it. But if Lucas pulls through, he'll confuse the girl into thinking he's a hero, and win Elvis's undying loyalty."

"Which he doesn't really want," Figgy says.

"Which he doesn't give a shit about," Sam says.

"He's a Pat Boone man," Figgy says.

"Exactly!"

Finished, I let out a big exhale and lean back. I can feel my heart beating in my neck.

"So that's the lot?" Sam asks.

"That's the lot."

Figgy turns to Sam and says, "No one will watch it."

I watch close for some indication that he's joking.

"Plus, it being all but unmakeable," Sam says back to Figgy.
My heart sinks.

"Licensing fees alone," Figgy says back.

So, no go. But what did I expect? What good do I deserve?
With Mom so ill, begging me to come home. Where I should
have gone a year ago! *More* than a year ago. But instead,
I'm here, playing make-believe with production companies.
Out of my element. Out of my mind. What the fuck?

"And this idea? It's outline-only, so far?" Figgy asks as he
and Sam sit identically. Their hands folded in front of them,
leaned forward on their elbows.

"Outline and treatment," I say.

"No script?"

"No script," I say, defeated.

Sam scratches at his beard. Then his hands go back, folded
before him.

"No one will watch it," Figgy says to me.

I don't shove my chair back. Or storm out. The angry
adrenaline I came in with has been used up in the pitch.
I appreciate that they were willing to hear me out. I feel like
I fought a good fight.

"Do ya live here?" Sam asks.

"San Francisco," I say. I look down and think of my mom,
without me, in St. Louis.

"And Ryan?"

"Same. We're roommates."

"Nice one," Sam says.

"No one will watch it," Figgy says to Sam.

"You said," I volunteer.

"*But*," Sam says to Figgy, then winks at me.

"Never really stopped us before," Figgy says.

"You around LA another day?" Sam asks.

"Until morning," I say, feeling unsure.

Figgy and Sam stand. I thank them for taking the time, and then I reach over the table to shake Figgy's hand. "We'll give you a bell," he says.

When I shake Sam's hand he says, "What he's saying is, don't fuck off just yet. We'll definitely call."

TEN

I STEP OUTSIDE INTO white-bright sun feeling elated. I pull out my phone to dial Ryan and right then my phone vibrates in my hand. A call from: **Blocked ID.**

I answer with an upbeat hello, and on the other end of the line Sarah says, quiet and distant and shy, "Hey. It's me."

My stunned response is, I hang up. And immediately wish I hadn't.

Then, again, my phone vibrates in my hand, and I jump. But this time it's just Ryan.

"This is fucked," I tell him.

"What's fucked?"

"Sarah just called me."

"What?" he says. "That's impossible."

My throat seizes.

"Dude, I can't imagine how hard this last year, year-plus, has been for you," Ryan says. "When you compound losing Sarah with feeling like you could have done more. I'm just really sorry."

When I'd called Ryan in London to tell him Sarah had jumped, his response was disbelief. I'd struggled to speak. My mouth opened, my throat clicked, and out poured a moaning cry that I've since come to understand as grief.

He offered to come, to get a flight out that night. But I told him not to. He told me to go somewhere. To be with people. I told him I would, but I didn't. Not for weeks.

Now, more than fifteen months later, Ryan's asking me, "Thomas? Is everything okay?"

I swallow hard, take a breath. "Yeah," I lie. "Yeah." And to distract before he asks anymore questions, I tell him, "I made the Anarchy pitch."

"Okay?" he says, jarred by my lack of segue. "They didn't hate it, did they? They seemed like they wouldn't hate it."

"They were effusive in their praise," I say. "They said they'd call."

"Don't kid. Are you kidding?" Ryan says, followed by a harsh, all-phlegm cough. I hear him exhale after a deep swallow.

"Are you feeling better?"

"Let's stay on one topic. This Anarchy news is huge."

"They asked if we had a script."

"What'd you tell them?" he asks.

"That we didn't."

"Shit," he says. "Did you tell them we've started it?"

"We haven't."

"Right, but... *Shit*. You should have told them... In the future, if it comes up, just say we have."

"Okay," I say, turning toward my car.

"Regardless, it's awesome," Ryan says. "I knew you'd kill it."

"You thought I'd blow it, and so did I."

"No, come on," he says. "I was only worried that you were still at Elsa's."

"*Elsa?*"

"The one with your phone?"

"Oh."

"We talked for half an hour. She's super rad. But more rad is what went down at Anarchy. You really just never know. You sure you're okay?"

"Yeah," I say blankly, though Sarah's call has me sideways.

"Then I'll call Peter now to relay the news."

"Okay," I say from what feels like a great distance.

I hang up. Then walk to my car in a trance.

ELEVEN

A T THE HOTEL, I exit the elevator on the third floor feeling fragile, and right there in the hallway is Sarah. Her hair is storm-tossed. Her lips impossible faded roses. Her skin so pale it looks see-through. She's crossed her arms so her hands grip her shoulders.

"I was so surprised when you called," I say. "I'm sorry I hung up."

Her brow goes dark with concern and her red-painted lips solder shut. She looks down then pulls a dry-erase marker from nowhere and writes on the inside of her left forearm, *Go home.*

"I can't," I say.

Sarah uses the inside of her right forearm to wipe clean the inside of her left. Then she walks past me into the elevator without a word or a touch. She pushes against its back wall, her head tilted down.

"I can go with you," I say. "We can get away from all this right off."

She looks at me point-blank while the doors close, doesn't make a move to stop it.

I mash the elevator button too late to open it back up, then hustle into the emergency exit, rush down the stairs.

By the time I'm on the ground floor, the doors are open, the elevator empty.

I get back in, take the elevator back up to the third floor. My shoulders tense as the doors open, hopeful she'll be there. But this time there's no Sarah.

I head to my room and sit on the bed with the door propped open, in case she comes back. Ryan calls twice, but I don't answer, fearful of distracting from this delicate moment.

Thirty minutes later, feeling emptied out, I have to muster the will to stand and head to EveryOther Films in Beverly Hills for my 3:30 p.m. meeting. The final pitch of the day.

TWELVE

IN DUSTY WHITE ETCHING, the door reads: EveryOther Films, Los Angeles Office. My mind's still in a haze when I walk in and am greeted by the receptionist—a young, twenty-three-year-old male pulled from a magazine ad whose spine is so straight, whose face is so symmetrical, I can't help but search for some flaw that will help me relax.

"You must be Ryan Ahearn. Or are you Thomas Muller?" he asks, chipper and without blinking.

"Mullen, actually, and I'm Thomas," I say, my energy zapped.

The receptionist, all smiles and daylight, says, "Oh, it says Muller here." He makes an adjustment on his touchscreen.

"Ryan won't be…" I start, but there's no need to finish because the receptionist offers a closed-mouth smile and tilts his head in a way that says, *Oh, poor Ryan!*

"It's no problem," he says, as he pokes and sweeps his touchscreen with a flourish. Then he presses a button that makes a muted *whoosh* sound. "Wait just one second." And that's how long it takes.

Out of the glass door to my left comes a woman in her late twenties, her hair a dishwater-blonde bob. The sleeves of her off-white silk blouse are rolled to the elbow. "Thomas? I'm Carly," she says, a genuine smile. She offers her right hand to shake and I see an elaborate tattoo peek out from the inside of her right forearm. I give her hand a firm squeeze. Her green eyes are highlighted by a delicate frame of black eyeliner.

"Have we met before?" Carly asks me.

"No," I say, certain we haven't. After Sarah, I spiraled. Then the move to San Francisco where I went from shut down to shut-in.

"Usually I can place people," she says, taking me in. "You don't live here?"

I shake my head.

"And you're not on TV?"

"Definitely not," I say with a snicker.

"Hmm. You're very familiar to me," she says, and realizes we're still shaking hands. "Oh, sorry!" Carly laughs and looks down at her iPad. "And Ryan couldn't make it?"

"He isn't well," I say.

"That's too bad," she says. "But it's great you're here, so welcome. If you can follow me."

Carly leads me through the door to the left of reception, then down a short, bleach-white hallway. I try to pull my shoulders back, to breathe deep, to find focus. But I don't want to be here. I'm on fumes after the early wake-up, plus the exclamation points of receiving mom's call, of seeing Sarah.

We arrive at a glass-doored meeting room. Inside there's a wide, glossy table lit with fluorescent tubes sunk into its glass top. Carly tells me I can have a seat. The big, cushy chairs recline with minimal effort.

"Would you like anything to drink?"

"Maybe a water?"

"On it," she says, then spins around and exits the room.

Agitated, I sit back and tell myself: just get through it. After this, the day is done. I try to relax by staring out at the never-ending city through two huge windows that take up an entire wall. I try to feel something about the landscape, but it's just buildings: beige and white and black and more beige. Topped by a flicked ash and aquamarine sky.

So my phone won't distract from my meeting with EveryOther's execs, I hold END until it shows a dorky, thirty-two-bit animation and powers off. I shove it in my pocket as Carly walks in and hands me a small bottle of Evian.

"You good?" she asks. I nod, but she doesn't look convinced. "You'll do great. They're just people, like anyone."

I nod again, this time a double-bob of my head.

"Good. So you know how this will go, in a minute you'll meet our three decision-making execs. You'll basically have ten minutes to impress them, and after that they'll probably have a few questions—five minutes at the absolute max. My advice, not that you need it, is just stay relaxed."

I am far from relaxed. All I can think is: head home. Don't bother pitching this meaningless movie about nothing to a trio of rich nobodies. While my mom is dying.

"And, y'know, knock 'em dead," she says. I down half the water in one gulp, put the cap back on, then set it down in front of me.

"Is there time for me to..."

"And here they are!" Carly says with maximum cheer, her words protecting me by resetting the room.

In single file, in walk three white men in blue suits, same haircut, same build, same expression, carrying identical notepads wrapped in leather binders. All as slick and rich-seeming as the entirety of this place. Each of the three shakes my hand and introduces himself. I don't quite hear the first man's name and am so thrown that the other names slip my mind, as if they never said them. Then we all sit. Across from the clones, my body's thermostat accelerates to bake.

Two of them say, in unison, "Let's get started." Then laugh at the fact that they've said it in unison. It relaxes me, and I start slow but not too slow, and move through the pitch, uninterrupted. They laugh when I hope they'll laugh, and widen their eyes when I hope they'll widen their eyes. I finish strong and tell them, "That's the lot."

"I get it," the one in the middle says.

The one on the left says, "It seems like you're afraid of it being violent."

"It's more of a cartoonish violence," I say. "If Lucas hits an alien hard enough so their pompadour wig flies off, they scurry back to their spaceship and stay there, ashamed to have disappointed Elvis. As he's their ultimate deity." They don't seem to love my response. "So as to the level of violence, think PG-thirteen."

"I'd rather not," the one on the right says, and laughs at his own joke.

"And guns?" asks the one in the center.

"No guns."

"I thought Elvis was a gun man," Center says.

"Elvis often carried a gun," I say. "But for this story, we feel like a lighter tone serves the story best."

"People won't get it," says Right.

"You make it subtle, and people think they're being made fun of," says Left. "And people don't like being made fun of."

"I feel like it'd be more timely if it took place at the White House," says Center.

"Excuse me?" I say.

"Well, in terms of translating globally, the White House is a place everyone's heard of," says Left.

"Over eight hundred thousand visitors a year," says Right.

I tell them Graceland has 650,000 visitors a year, and mention that, more importantly, Elvis has nothing to do with the White House, outside a drop-in during the Nixon Administration.

"True, *true*," says Center. "But by all accounts, Louis is just dropping into Graceland, so it's largely the same thing, right?"

"Lucas," I correct. "And, well, not exactly…"

"The aliens are terrorists, is my point," Center says.

"*Terrorists*," says Right. "I like it."

"Topical," says Left.

"And why wouldn't they want to steal the White House instead?" Center says.

"Especially when Elvis is visiting," says Left. "That's a true score!"

"Nothing unites an audience like a common enemy," says Center. "And these terrorists would give them one."

"Extra-terror-*estrial*…" says Right.

"Love it," says Left.

"Though maybe it's not a film," Center says.

"Go on," says Left.

"I just feel like maybe it's a video game," says Center. "Or even an app."

"An app?" I say, as Carly walks by outside. She looks through the half-frosted window. I don't know if she can read the dispirited look on my face.

"Are they still making lunch boxes?" Center asks. "If so, this is definitely lunch box material."

"A toy line is in this project's future," Right says.

"At least a Nerf gun featuring Elvis-saving velcro-tipped darts," Left says. "Those things don't stick to satin jumpsuits!"

Center looks at Left and Right, then checks his very expensive-looking watch and asks if I'll excuse them for just one second.

"Sure," I say.

"If you could just step outside."

"Oh! Okay, yeah." I make my way out of the room.

In the hallway, Carly approaches. "Everything okay?"

"Let's say yes?"

She makes a face that says she's sorry. "I don't know what's happening in there, but you need to believe in your idea. Don't fold." She looks in the room, then behind her before turning back to me. "What I mean is, I've been in that room before. Don't let them manipulate you. It's...kind of their thing."

"You mean they change everything about your idea until it makes no sense, *then* suggest a toy line?"

"Uhh, yeah," she says, a pained expression.

I let out a hard exhale.

"You good?"

I shrug, tell her, "I guess."

She looks in the room, then back at me.

"They're ready for you," Carly says, and waves to them through the glass. "Good luck."

I head back in.

"Please sit," says Center, so I sit. "We've reviewed your idea and while it raises some immediate questions, we'll be in touch with your agent right away about the possibility of moving forward."

"Really?" I ask, genuinely shocked, and also unsure of what idea, exactly, they'd be calling about.

"Absolutely," Right says.

"Thank you so much for coming in," Left says.

They stand, so I do, and next we're all shaking hands. Suddenly, these men love me. Which is so confusing. Still, I force a smile, and while my hand is being bobbed and squeezed, I look out to see Carly through the glass, a disappointed expression, then an eyebrow raise that I read as, *Told you.*

THIRTEEN

CARLY WALKS ME TO reception, where the smiley male receptionist validates my parking with a joy before unseen.

Carly leads me to the exit. "And last time, I promise, but we've seriously never met?"

"Sorry."

"No, I'm sorry to keep asking. Thanks again for coming in."

I turn my phone back on as I head out of EO's glass double doors, and while it comes back to life, I press the elevator's down button. I call Ryan back. He answers right as the elevator doors open. As I step inside I tell him, "My mother is dying."

After a breath he asks, "What the fuck are you talking about? Didn't you tell me a year ago she passed?"

I press P1 as the doors close. "I mean, what the f—" he starts. But the signal's gone. We've disconnected. "I'll call you back," I tell the dead line.

❖❖❖

I EXIT EVERYOTHER'S UNDERGROUND parking elevator, and I stop when I see a text from Ryan:

This mom shit is a huge baffling bummer and i'm worried/ angry/worried.

There's no time to consider a response, because Elsa is there, waiting for me with crossed arms.

"I know," she says, quiet, and shuffles over. "Ryan told me everything. I know. Okay?"

When I step forward like she's not there, she follows. From behind, me Elsa says, "I know all about Sarah."

"Know what?" I snap, turning to face her.

"How it ended. That she jumped. And I'm sorry."

Ryan and his big fucking mouth.

"Why are you here?" I challenge, looking at her dead-on.

"Ryan said this is where you'd be."

"So?" I say, and throw my arms up. "You don't just show up!"

"He asked me to come check on you."

"Well, I'm *fine*," I say.

"I'm just trying to help."

"Well, fucking stop!"

I turn and head to my car.

"I'm sorry I pretended to be Sarah!" Elsa says, continuing to follow. We've known each other a few hours and she's already resurrecting skeletons from our past. "I'm even sorrier about your mom's cancer."

Which sets me off. "How do you know that?" I ask as I turn and step toward her with barely-controlled fury. Fury at her for being here. At Ryan for telling her anything. "Did you call her after I left?!"

Elsa looks down.

"What is *wrong* with you?!"

"I didn't tell her I wasn't Sarah."

"Oh, my fucking god!" I shout, and turn away from her. I hurry to my rental car with balled fists.

"And what's wrong with *me*?" she shouts.

Not far off, car tires whine as they grip the parking structure's gray-painted floor.

"You're so incredibly self-absorbed," Elsa says behind me. "You're not even asking how she is!" I lengthen my strides. Behind me Elsa says, "Thomas? *Thomas*?!"

I turn to tell her, "*Quit* saying my name."

As I open the door to my car, she says, "Please talk to me."

I do not like her here. Pressing me on my mother. Acting like Sarah's all-the-way gone. Making me feel exposed.

My phone rings, and I pull it out. **Blocked ID.**

"It's Sarah," I say, holding up my phone, defiant.

"I don't think it is," Elsa says.

I dip hard into my car and slam the door closed before I answer. "Hello?"

"Don't hang up," Sarah says.

I take a sharp, quick breath. "I won't."

"I just want to know how you're doing."

"You saw."

"I what? This connection is terrible," she says, and pauses. I check my phone, which goes from two bars to one, then put it back to my ear. Her voice echoes. The connection teeters.

"Just tell me where you are," I say.

"Sorry, what?" she says.

"Tell me, and I'll come."

"You're cutting out."

Then the *beep-beep-beep* of the call ending.

As I wait for her to call back, I grip the wheel hard as I watch Elsa recede toward, then into, the elevator. By the time I exit the garage I have four missed calls:

Blocked ID.

Blocked ID.

Blocked ID.

Mom.

❖❖❖

I'M TWO BLOCKS AWAY when the signal's strong enough for me to dial in to check the single voicemail. A message that's only two words. My mother's weakened voice saying, simply, "Please, Thomas."

FOURTEEN

ONCE I'M INSIDE MY hotel room, I call Ryan.

"What is happening?" I ask him, angry.

"I want to ask you the same thing."

"You sent Elsa to EO Games! I mean, what the fuck?"

"She asked where you were, and I told her," he says. "She was concerned. *I'm* concerned."

"Thanks, but if we could keep ambushes to a minimum, I'd be grateful."

"Well, it's not my fault that you're not being straight with me!" he says, voice strained.

"You told her about Sarah," I say, exasperated, disappointed.

"Well…yeah."

"It's not okay," I say. "I don't know her."

"She said Sarah called while you were in the parking garage—why would you say that?"

Which is when my call waiting bleeps, a **646** area code.

"One sec," I tell him, relieved by the interruption. "Other line."

"*Dude,*" he says.

I click over and after a hello I hear, "Hey, it's Carly from EO Games—you free tonight?"

"Tonight?" I say, surprised by the invite.

"Can you do Thirsty Crow on Sunset? At eight?"

"I can do eight."

"Cool," she says. "See ya." And hangs up.

I click back over, and distract Ryan by telling him, "That was Carly from EveryOther. She wants to meet up later."

"I don't care about that right now."

"Well, they said they'd be calling Peter."

"I need to know about your mom," Ryan says. I close my eyes slowly. After too long a silence, he says, "I'm your best friend. Tell me what's going on."

I lean against the desk and kick off my shoes. I can't figure quite how to start. With my phone pressed hot against my ear, I track back to when I lied to Ryan, via email. If he knew the truth, he'd demand I go home. And if I went home, then I'd have to confront the limitless sadness of my mother gone.

I swallow deep, ready to speak but then there's the *hiss-hiss-hiss* of cat scratches at my door.

"Fuck, dude," I say. "You told her where I was staying?"

"Who?"

"*Elsa.*"

"What?" he says. "No."

Annoyed, I head to the door. "Unbelievable," I say.

As I pull the phone away from my face, I hear Ryan say, "I swear I didn't…"

When I answer the door, I see he's telling the truth. It's not Elsa. I clap my phone closed without another word and my mouth goes immediately dry. Because, like an angel, Sarah's gliding past me, into the room.

FIFTEEN

I'M STANDING, PRESSED AGAINST the window, while Sarah sits on the bed's edge. Her dress is navy flowers on white.

"You came back," I say.

Sarah nods.

"After so long."

On her left arm, in dry-erase marker, she draws four parallel lines, then a diagonal slash through them. Then again. When she starts on the third set of parallel lines, I guess that she's counting the time since she stood on the ledge of my Brooklyn rooftop.

"Fifteen months," I say. "I get it."

Sarah wipes her arm clean and takes a lazy look around the room. Her gaze lands on a halo of fading sunlight on the wall. The room is filled with remedial shapes.

"How are you here?"

Sarah looks at me, annoyed. She erases her arm then writes, *Don't ask dumb questions.*

"At least talk to me?" I ask.

She erases her arm except for the words *dumb questions.* She writes, *I just said.* Then underlines *just* and circles *dumb questions.*

Fearing she'll leave too soon, I push myself forward, take a step toward her and reach out with my hand. Sarah evades by sliding soundlessly off the bed and backing away in the direction of the door.

"I'll take you to dinner," I say weakly.

Angry, she wipes her arm clean then jabs at her arm with the pen, scrawling out, *Your mother.*

"If I don't go home, she can get better."

She leans back, exasperated. Without erasing, she writes, *NO.*

Now she backs farther away, her gray eyes on me.

"If I go home, she dies."

Coward, she writes. With her back to the door.

"Please don't go," I say.

She slashes at her left forearm with her right to do a quick-erase, then writes in thick dry-erase ink: *Close your eyes.*

"No," I plead.

She underlines each word with three harsh stabs. *Close. Your. Eyes.*

"If I do, you'll go," I say.

She stares at me, exhales a soundless sigh.

"Fine," I say. I stand up straight, put my feet wide, then close my eyes.

When I open them back up, I'm right: Sarah's gone.

❖ ❖ ❖

IT'S TEN MINUTES LATER when I'm on the edge of my bed, trying to calm myself, and my phone rings loud in my pocket. A call from Ryan.

"Seriously, no more bullshit," he says, clearly frustrated. "Can you tell me what's going on with your mom? Or not? Just one or the other, and I'll stop asking."

I consider the tangled logic, the embarrassing effort of explaining that if he'd known, he would have joined Sarah's chorus, demanding I go home. And now, I expect he'll do the same. "Not," I say.

Ryan let's out a sound of disgust. "I'm your best friend." His voice is gauzy with disappointment.

"It's complicated."

"Your *dead* mother is alive and now dying?" he says. "What's complicated about that?"

I go quiet.

It's maybe thirty seconds of silence before Ryan, defeated, says to me, "I'm sorry, but this whole thing? I don't get it. And I keep thinking back to when I moved, and how clear it was that you were struggling. But I used a strategy I picked up in London: ignore it until it goes away. But it's not letting up, and now all this with your mom."

"I need to go," I say.

"Fuck, man, seriously?" Ryan says.

"I think I better call home."

"Oh," Ryan says. "Okay. Well, I'm here."

Off the phone with Ryan, I dial my parents' landline. After three rings, my father answers.

"It's me," I say.

"It's dire times over here, Thomas."

I try to tell him I can't face it, but my throat's seized up. No words come out.

"I'll put your mother on."

I hear the exchange. Dad whispers my name to Mom. Mom whispers, "Oh, thank heavens."

"Thomas?" she says to me.

"Mom," I say, a gasp that ekes out of my closing throat.

"It's okay," she says.

I lean my head back to keep from losing it.

"It's okay," she says again, her weak voice cracking.

But it's not okay. If I stay away, maybe. But if I go home, it won't ever be, again.

"It's okay," she says. "It's okay."

Then Dad gets back on the line.

"Son?" he says.

"Yeah?" I whisper.

"All I'm saying is hurry."

SIXTEEN

TWENTY-TWO MONTHS AGO, I was home alone in Brooklyn when my mom called and said, "Thomas?"

"Hey, Mom."

"Are you sitting?"

With an opening like that, I knew sitting wouldn't do any good. I clenched my stomach, hoping the news would be bad but not awful.

"What's going on?" I asked.

"There's a spot on my lung," she said. "It's the size of a stone that was the size of a pinpoint. Doctors say it will grow to the size of my lung. I want you to come home."

I was under contract for the rest of the week, but I called and told them my mother was ill. Then I flew home to St. Louis.

❖❖❖

MY PARENTS PICKED ME up from the airport, and we went straight to my mother's doctor.

The doctor said to my mom, "As yours is an advanced case, we hope to see the metastatic deposits in your liver and in your bones shrink significantly, or totally melt away."

"Her liver?" I interrupted. "Her *bones*?"

Her lung was just the starting point. The place in her body where they first discovered it.

The doctor went on, "It's important to understand that intensive chemotherapy—even a bone marrow transplant— won't kill off every cancer cell in your body. Plus, there's your age to consider. There's no case of absolute success, it's just remission we're talking about here. Let's stray from the word 'cured.'"

The doctor didn't have charts. He didn't have X-rays. He was just a tie, rolled sleeves, and a beard. He said, "Best case scenario: the cancer becomes merely parasitic. We quell it with therapy, hope it stays down for months and if we're fortunate, a year or maybe even several years."

"And worst case?" my dad asked.

The doctor looked at my mother apologetically. "The cancer resists everything we've got, even the experimental stuff, while the treatment weakens you considerably and your quality of life dips drastically."

I found myself in a state of absolute awareness. I watched my mother, my safety net who protected me my whole life, to see if she'd shrink to nothing under the buzzing office lights.

The doctor's sleeved elbows were on his knees, his hands woven together, thick black hair on the back of each of his fingers. How many times had he told people they would die? The light in the room made it so there weren't any shadows.

I waited for Mom's reaction. But so far there wasn't one.

"Is she going to die?" I blurted, her only child, afraid my family would soon be halved.

"Statistics don't tell you what is going to happen to any one person, just groups," the doctor said.

The statistics: more than 70 percent of people with my mother's condition die within two years.

"'*More* than seventy percent'?" I said. "How many more?"

"Thomas," my father said.

And the doctor said, "Blah, blah, blah." Abstractions and ambiguities, all.

My mother reached over to hold my hand.

"Are you okay?" I asked her. "I want you to be okay."

"I love you so much," she said, and kissed my hand. "I need you to be strong for what happens next."

I felt weightless.

❖❖❖

IN THE CAR ON the way home from the hospital, my mother, confident and composed, told my father and I, "I'd like for you two to assist my suicide."

My stomach sucked in, my throat seized.

"Oh, honey," my father said to my mother, his voice so gentle. He reached over and placed his right hand on the back of her neck.

A wave of heat rocketed through me.

"Mom," I said. "What about chemo?"

We both watched my mother.

"You heard the doctor," she said. "And at my age."

"You're only sixty-one!" I said.

Mom looked straight ahead at the street and sidewalk and trees that hurried past us.

"*Mom*," I insisted.

"It *could* go away with treatment," Dad said.

"It won't," she said.

"But it could!" I cried. "You don't know."

"I know."

"You don't," I pleaded. "Don't be selfish!"

"*Thomas*," my father said, so I'd stand down.

"No," she said. "No chemotherapy."

I began to throw up in the back seat. There was so much of it, my father had to pull the car over.

When I stopped, I saw my mother was doubled over in the front seat. Her hands over her face.

"Mom," I said. *"Please."* Wet hung from my lips. Neither of us could stop crying.

"Enough," my father turned and said to me. I could count on one hand the times I saw my father angry, but he was angry now. "Goddammit!" he shouted at the windshield, his voice tense with pent-up hurt. I didn't look at him. I just looked at the floorboard, the impossible amount of sick that had forced its way out of me, then closed my eyes. I choked back a sob, which turned into a loud, gulping swallow. Then I pushed a quick breath out of my nose, eliciting twin rockets of vomit and snot. I wiped my mouth and nose with my sleeve, and sat up.

After another minute, calm prevailed—or at least quiet. At some point, my father drove on. When we hit the speed limit, I let go and sat back. The nasty film of hydrochloric acid was on my tongue, and an empty, nowhere feeling pulsed all through me.

"Son," my father said. "If your mother wants to die, we need to let her die."

Mom took Dad's hand and kissed it.

To keep her alive, I knew I had to leave and not come back. But I didn't say a word. No one did. We drove with the windows down to help dilute the smell. After a while, my mother, without looking back, reached between the seats and rested her left hand on my knee.

SEVENTEEN

I'M TWENTY MINUTES EARLY to meet Carly at the Thirsty Crow. After I locate it in a squashed clump of unremarkable shop fronts, I pull into a parking spot two blocks clear. I sit for a minute, then force myself to call Ryan.

"You called your mom?"

I watch the bright, recurring blot of headlights arrive, then vanish in snapshot clicks, followed by the wheeze of taillights in gentler red.

"I did."

"And you're going home?" he asks. I shake my head, though no one can see it. "Because now you have to."

"This is why I didn't tell you," I say. The glands in my neck tingle, a signal that floodgates inside me are trying to break open. If I stay away, there's a chance she's okay. If I go, though... So I shut it all down. "Right now," I tell Ryan, with finality, "I just can't face it."

I wait for him to speak, but all I can hear is the light scratch of cell phone connection. The weight of Ryan's silence pushes down on me, makes my shoulders ache. Then it pushes into me and it settles hard and hot and heavy in my belly. So I hang up.

❖❖❖

THE THIRSTY CROW IS a cramped, boisterous hotspot with a speakeasy feel. I find a pair of stools along the bend of the horseshoe-shaped bar under a light bulb so dim I double take when I realize it isn't candlelight. After a few minutes of decompressing, one of the bartenders—a black guy with a beard, suspenders, sleeves rolled up—asks, "What can I get you?"

I point blindly at a battered, paper cocktail menu, all the drinks described in ten-point font. "I'll try this."

"The Mezcaline Smash?"

"That's the one," I say with an assured nod.

Once he turns to make it, I squint at the menu to see that I've ordered a drink designed by Rahad Coulter-Stevenson that mixes El Silencio mezcal, green chartreuse, lemon, mint, agave, and Peychaud's. Some ingredients I've heard of, most I have no idea what they'll taste like. All of which I'm grateful for, so everything can just *slow down.*

My drink arrives on a black napkin two minutes later and I hand the bartender my credit card. He makes a throat-slashing gesture with his right hand and mouths, "Close it out?" I shake my head so he'll leave it open.

The Mezcaline Smash tastes smoky and tart and burns the bottom of my throat, but it's just fine. I hold my fingers around it, taking occasional swallows, while I stare into space. When Carly's not there seventeen minutes later, I decide that if she doesn't show up, so be it. After Sarah, I learned to drink alone just fine. I learned to drink alone, no problem.

Then Carly whirlwinds in and says, "Sorry I'm late. My Uber driver ignored his GPS, so it was a circus of wrong turns."

I say I didn't know she was late and she tells me I'm sweet.

I watch as she musses her hair then sheds her oxblood-colored leather jacket. It's Carly, clearly, but not the same Carly from earlier. Away from her workplace surroundings, there's a shimmer to her. I feel myself sit up in response.

"What'd you order?" she asks.

I point at the menu, flat on the bar. "This one." Then I slide my drink toward her. "Want to try?"

She takes a soft sip, then waves the bartender over. When he arrives, she points at my drink and says, "One of those feisty things." Then tells me, "So, EO's going to make an offer."

"Wow. Seriously?"

"They suck," she says.

"Oh," I say.

Her drink arrives and Carly leans to access money in her front pocket, but I tell the bartender, "Put it on mine."

"Thank you," she says with a smile, followed by a sidelong glance, before she goes back to sniping at EO. "And I'm sorry. I don't mean to bum you out. An offer's great. But that place is such a dud."

"So you invited me here to tell me not to accept?" I ask.

"I invited you here to warn you," she says. "The only reason to do a deal with EO is if you're just in it for the money. Which, maybe you are."

With my bank account's current state of affairs, I might have to be. These drinks are twelve dollars a pop, plus the expense of being here at all: the Uber to SFO; the flight here; the rental car; the hotel for a night.

"But," Carly says, and slugs down half her drink, "here's the shitty plot twist. EO makes offers like this all the time to block competitors from accessing good ideas. But if by some miracle, The Clone Trio *does* make something totally lunatic with your premise as a jumping-off point, you'll get nothing in the way of credit. And if you try to use your original idea after that, in any form, they'll sue the shit out of you. It's their favorite hobby."

"Yikes," I say.

"Yeah," Carly says. "Drives you to drink." She guzzles down the rest of hers. "Another?"

"Sure," I say. With an EO offer pending, I can risk putting myself a little further in debt.

When the bartender passes, she points to our glasses and tells him, "The same."

❖❖❖

CARLY HURRIES THROUGH HER second drink and, now tipsy, her interest in me is amplified. She fires off a string of rapid-fire questions. "Why did you move from New York City to San Francisco? Besides the fact that the winters there are brutal nonsense. But why not LA? Oh, but first who was the agent that set a meeting with EO's bigwigs?"

I respond by asking, "Do you meet to discourage everyone who's getting an offer?"

"Never," Carly shrugs.

"Then why me?"

"Because it's annoying the shit out of me that I can't figure out where we met."

"Because we haven't?"

Carly waves this off with one hand. Then all of her quiets, and she runs a finger along the side of her sweating glass. "Plus, I'm a little sad," she says. "And maybe you seemed a little sad, too."

Carly raises her drink, and holds it out in front of her.

"To spilling my guts," she says. "And to throwing you under the bus." I raise my glass to hers so they clink. "And while I'm on a roll, I don't mean to come off all bratty and condescending about EO. It's just they have so much money to buy up good ideas, but then they bury them or turn them into their crappier ideas."

"Why don't you quit?"

"And miss the chance to be the company's under-empowered, self-righteous moral center?" She laughs. "No chance! Plus, the pay is stupid good."

◆◆◆

CARLY'S NEARLY THROUGH HER third drink, and I'm only halfway through my second when she asks why Ryan wasn't there. "A creative partner falling out?"

"Not at all," I tell her. "He really is sick."

I explain that we're best friends, and how he showed up after being away in London, and how grateful I was that he did, the both of us heartbroken, and me, especially, needing the support. Needing a boost. And then our Elvis idea came about, and how it landed me here, on this stool, in this city, on this night.

"What's her name?" she asks.

"Who?"

"The heartbreak initiator you've been carrying around."

"Sarah," I say.

"Sarah. *Sarah.*" Like it's a flavor her mouth is trying to figure out. Her brow creases and she looks away. Then she relaxes and takes a finishing swallow of her drink.

"Jake," she says and puts her glass down hard.

"Jake?"

"That's the butthole that head-fucked my heart," Carly says with a laugh. I laugh, too. She licks her lips and starts to giggle. "Where are you staying?"

"A hotel on Franklin," I say.

"The 101 Cafe?"

"The one above it."

"Let's go there and eat a BLT."

"Now?"

"Twenty minutes ago," she says. I take a second to let the moment register. "Oh, just say yes. I'm a fucking joy."

Carly stands and trips back, but catches my arm to save herself from a drunken tumble.

"See!?" she says, then laughs hard, thanks me for the save, and surprises me with a kiss on the cheek. Then she waves down the bartender who delivers the bill. I sign it and follow her to the exit.

EIGHTEEN

THREE WEEKS AFTER SARAH stood on the ledge of my roof, I was eating alone at a restaurant. I was eating all of my meals alone then, followed by going home alone and sitting alone. No movies, no video games, I would sit. Focus on DVR'd television commercials that lived between meaningless, candy-coated sitcom storylines and false dramas. I preferred the commercials because they served as a guide. What was I supposed to eat now that Sarah was gone? They were happy to tell me. What was I supposed to drink now? They weren't shy. What kind of car should I own now? Enough commercials and I knew.

I knew which shampoo would make my hair an easy-to-style silk. What motor oil would best synthetically lubricate the car I didn't own. Which brand of adult diaper would best fit my needs. What beer would triumphantly lead to an island of bikini'd women. Which pizza would bring me closer to God. What kind of life I was supposed to live.

But within all of these, I couldn't find the commercial that answered: What was I going to do now that Sarah wasn't coming back and nothing I could do would change it? No commercials offered an explanation. But if I wanted a son of a bitch of a truck with a four-ton payload, I knew whom to call.

Those days, nothing had flavor. I was head-down at a restaurant that was walking distance from my Brooklyn Heights apartment, halfway through chili that tasted like peppered candle wax. Right after I'd taken a bite of cornbread that sat on my tongue like polluted air, Sarah was standing across the table from me. My fork dropped from my hand. All the moisture vanished from my mouth.

"My God," I said. Seeing Sarah, after never thinking I'd see her again, made my whole body go wonky. I squinted, trying to find the truth. "This isn't possible."

Her eyes glowed with sad wonder as she wrote on the inside of her right forearm with a dry-erase marker. Then she showed me: *And yet.*

Which raced me back to three years before, at a party in the West Village. Sarah walked in and the room tilted in her direction. My breath stuttered, afraid she'd be lured away. But I got to her first. I shook her hand. Before she'd even said hello: I knew.

She quietly told me that it was her first night out in a while. A few weeks before her thirty-four-year-old brother had passed, cardiac arrest in the night that killed him in seconds, and since the funeral she'd been lying low. But now she needed to talk about him, about it. Then asked if I had any brothers or sisters. When I told her I was an only child she said, *Thank god. Any more dead siblings and I'm going to lose it.*

The apartment we were in was full, but it felt like no one else was around. This was before. When my mother was in perfect health.

Later, we were standing in the kitchen. I asked if I could call her and she told me she wasn't putting her number in a flip phone. She pulled an Expo dry-erase marker off the refrigerator. Then wrote my number on her arm. A week later, she called. A week after that, she spent the night for the first time. Weeks later, we fell, I thought, invincibly, in love.

Two years later, she was gone.

But now, in this restaurant, somehow Sarah was across from me again. Her arm stained with the words, *And yet.*

The moment was undercut by some loudmouth at the table behind me who was using profanity like commas: "So this fucking dog won't eat the fucking treat. Bullshit! Stupid little fucker. I said, trade in that dinky-ass toy fucking poodle for a fucking pit bull, already."

I swallowed deep and told Sarah, "This is all my fault."

She wrote on her arm, *This was my decision.* She underlined *my.*

"Oh, and don't get me started on video games," the loudmouth said. "The other day, I walk in and see my fucking son pull a cab driver out of this fucking car then shoot the son of a bitch in the goddamn face with the touch of a fucking button."

His *fucking* son?

"Video games are bullcrap," his wimpy friend agreed.

"Fucking-a-right. I don't need him learning to shoot a goddamn rocket launcher into the base of a fucking building to get a high score."

Sarah eased into the chair across from me, coiling one leg under her, while the other stretched to the hardwood of the restaurant floor.

I took the deepest possible breath, but couldn't speak. She erased her arm, then wrote, *What now?*

"I can't go home," I told her.

She shook her head, then started to rise up.

"*Wait,*" I said.

The waiter stopped. "I'm sorry?" I waved him away as Sarah got to her feet, ready to go.

"I'll do anything so you'll come back."

On her arm she wrote, *Prove it.*

"How?" I begged. She was backing away.

Rosemary, she wrote. My mother's name.

"He's going to go fucking brain-dead if he keeps playin' them shittin' games."

I turned around to The Fucking Man and said, "Hey. *Hey.*" He looked at me. "Could you shut the fuck up?"

"*Excuse* me?" he said.

I turned back to Sarah, who was nearly gone.

"Sarah. *Please.*"

"Fucking *excuse* me."

I'd have given anything to lure her back. Almost anything.

"Hey, you little *fucking* prick."

There was no way I could go home.

Now The Fucking Man was out of his chair and in front of mine. His jet-black hair was slicked back. There were hard lines surrounding his mouth. He pushed me in the face with his wide, sweaty hand. I wiped my face with my sleeve then looked up at him obstinate. He pulled his right arm back, then hit me hard across the face. I heard a woman yelp while I was swung hard to my right. I tried to brace myself, but all I accomplished was to wipe the dishes and silverware nearest me off the table resulting in shatter, splatter, and pings. When I tried to correct, I went too far and slumped off the left side of my chair at the feet of The Fucking Man.

He stood over me. I looked up at him to see beads of sweat all around his mouth. His lips pressed into a frown. Droplets of snot steamed from his nostrils. He looked ridiculous. I started to laugh for the first time in weeks.

"You think that's fucking funny, you little fuck?"

I nodded. I was dizzy, and wished Sarah was still here.

"Fuck you, you piece of fuck," he said and backed away.

Piece of *fuck*? I laughed!

The Fucking Man turned back toward me. I heard his friend squeak, "Bobby, come on."

My body was propped against my chair when he hit me across the face a second time. The force of the blow sent the chair spinning away, and me onto my back.

A woman's voice: "Oh my *god.*"

Metallic blood ran like a spigot onto my tongue. I tried to spit it at The Fucking Man, but it fell out of my mouth and ran hot down my chin.

I blinked slowly. I was struggling to stay conscious. When my eyes closed, all over again, Sarah was flying. I could see it. Her dress's rapid, slapping ripple. Arms wide and her head turned hard to the right. Her entire body tilting slowly away from me with impossible grace.

Before everything went black.

NINETEEN

A S I DRIVE US to the 101 Cafe, Carly's primly seated: straight spine, hands crossed in lap. She stares out the window as we zip past tree-fronted homes beneath a lead sky streaked with cirrus.

"When's your flight?" she asks.

"Tomorrow afternoon."

"Hm," she says. "Good."

She smiles and shifts subtly in her seat.

A minute later, Carly looks over at me like she's searching for some flaw.

"What?" I ask.

"We've seriously never met?" she says.

"If I say yes, will you stop asking?"

She laughs and gives my shoulder a soft shove, then looks out her passenger-side window.

When my phone rings on the console, Carly says, "I'll get it!" and picks up my phone with a laugh.

"Blocked ID?" she says, and I freeze as a cool of sweat covers my entire body.

"Oh, shit," she says. "Is this Sarah?"

"Please," I say, and grip the wheel hard. "Don't."

She sets the phone back in the console in a hurry. "I wouldn't *ever*," she says, and reaches over and touches my arm.

I swallow deep, trying to catch my breath. "I'm sorry," I say.

"It's okay," she says. "It's all okay. All this *after* stuff sucks."

❖ ❖ ❖

I PARK IN THE hotel's open-air parking structure, and as we both get out, I sneak a peek at my Missed Calls to see: **Blocked ID**. I quick-scan in every direction, searching for Sarah. There's no sign, but I seize up at the thought of being with Carly, while Sarah's in the lobby, or the restaurant, or outside the elevator, waiting.

"What?" Carly says, waiting for me at the back of the car.

"There's something I haven't told you."

"Well, there's *tons* I haven't told you." She comes toward me.

"But Sarah," I say from another planet entirely.

"But *Jake*," she says, like it's a game. She stops right in front of me and say, "Hey. Hey." Demanding my attention.

The second I give it to her, she grabs my face and kisses me. The kiss is reckless and full and wet. Before I think to withdraw—what if Sarah sees?—Carly eases away, smiling. Then she pulls my arm like it's kite string and leads me toward the sliding glass doors of the lobby.

Inside, as Carly leads me down the short stairs to the 101 Cafe, spindles of panic let loose in my lungs. I try to pull away from our hand-in-hand, but she holds on tight and gives me a fun but fierce, "*No*." After a beat she tells me, "God, I'm hilarious, especially when I'm drunk."

Once we're under the soft, dim light of the packed restaurant, walking on waxed beige linoleum spotted with speckles of red and brown, I scan every face present in the leather booths and leather-backed stools, a search for Sarah.

At the end of the counter, a man with a beard that's squared at the bottom says he's sorry, but it'll be at least a twenty-minute wait.

"We're staying in the hotel," Carly says. "Can we take it to our room? Or have it sent up?"

"Sure," the host says, and hands her a menu.

Without looking she asks, "Do you have BLTs?"

"Yep. Avocado?"

"Yes! And two orders of pancakes." Carly scans the menu, then flips it. "And two glasses of champagne." Then she asks me, "Two okay?"

Concerned by how much all this will cost, I still tell her, "Two's great."

"No, four," she tells the host. Then asks me, "Four, yeah?" She puts her hand on my chest and says, "I'm getting this. You got drinks."

I don't see Sarah anywhere.

◆◆◆

OUTSIDE THE ELEVATOR, CARLY lights the button for the elevator with her knuckle, which flashes me back to earlier on. It puts me on high alert, a renewed panic: Sarah might be inside.

"It's just three floors," I say and make a move to take the stairs.

But then the ding of the elevator's arrival and Carly says, "Right on time."

When the brushed-silver doors open, and there's no one inside, I expel a hurried exhale, then stand stiff in the back corner.

"You're such a weirdo," Carly says, leaning casually against the sidewall.

The doors open at the third floor. If Sarah's out there, I want Carly to go first, to create enough distance between us for plausible deniability.

But then she asks me, "Which way?"

My first thought is: let the doors close, go back downstairs. Start over without Carly on the ground floor. But I point to the right without saying a word, so Carly goes to the right. But when I don't immediately follow, she says, "Thomas? You coming?"

The jig is up. I sheepishly step forward out of the elevator into stark, harsh light. I look right, then left, into the empty, soundless hallway.

Sarah, much to my relief, much to my disappointment, is nowhere to be seen. And Carly, welcoming, awaits.

TWENTY

I WAKE IN THE middle of the night to the whispering hiss of Sarah's *scratch-scratch-scratches* at my hotel door. My heart goes into overdrive—Carly's naked and asleep against me, breathing. Battling a rush of shame, a sense that I've cheated, I ease away from Carly without a word and tiptoe to the room's front door. I open it with deft, quiet care. In the low-lit hallway, all haze and wonder, there's Sarah: her face unblemished beauty, eyes gray and infinite.

I stand aside, and in she walks.

In the bathroom, I thumb toward the wall that separates us from Carly. I tell Sarah, "I don't *know* her."

Sarah, who's sitting on the counter next to a dry, white washcloth covered in my toiletries, looks at me like, *Yeah, right.*

"We were drunk," I say. "And nothing happened."

Sarah nods at the trash can. In the bathroom's blinding light, it's easy to see a torn condom wrapper caught on the edge of a thin, translucent trash bag.

I take a moment to soak in the bathroom's details—the baby-blue fixtures, the white and off-white checkered floor, a spot of toothpaste on the mirror—so later I can remember this moment for maximum despair.

"I'm sorry," I say. "But she's no one to me."

Sarah recoils, makes a face. On her arm she writes, *Don't be mean.*

"I just want you to understand."

Sarah's face softens. She erases her arm, then lets out a mute exhale. Then she writes, *I understand just fine.*

Desperate for clarity, I ask her, "Understand what?"

Sarah erases. Then writes, *That you're still here.* She slides off the counter and moves toward the closed door.

"No," I say. *"Please."*

Sarah underlines *you're* and *still* and *here*, then drops her arms to her side like she's given up.

I move past her and open the door. The hot, concentrated light of the bathroom spills into the black room, tinged with the scent of maple syrup from last night's late-night meal.

"Thomas?" Carly whispers from bed.

I don't mean to, but I react with a quick *shush* I'm able to almost quell.

Sarah's dusty eyes lock on to mine, she gives a look like, *Go get her, tiger.* Then she backs toward the door, and shows what she's written on her arm: *If you won't go, then I will.*

"Sorry I fell asleep," Carly says.

Where? I mouth to Sarah, as I open the door.

HOME, she writes.

My face goes slack and my lungs empty. A tingle spreads in my jaw—an early warning I might throw up. Then Sarah steps forward, steps out. She exits without looking back, then she's gone.

"What time is it?" Carly says. I hear her sit up, the rustle of sheets and blankets. I let the door auto-close and wait for the metal-on-metal scrape of hotel room door parts to click shut. "Is everything okay?"

The door closes and I tell Carly, "Maybe."

When I turn off the bathroom light, there's a flash of white before everything goes immediately, impossibly black.

"You sure?" she asks, a voice in utter dark.

Hands out in front of me, I move toward the bed guided by a single, slim blur of streetlamp light that's tricked its way through a narrow crack in the curtains. When my knees gently meet the foot of the king-size bed, Carly turns on a small reading lamp bolted into the headboard. The bedspread is clamped between her arms to cover her breasts. A look of concern on her face that might be fear.

"That was Sarah," I say.

"She called?"

"She was here."

"I didn't hear her."

"She doesn't really speak, anymore."

Carly's eyes squint as she juts her head forward and slightly to the side. She searches my face for clues. "I'm not sure what that means," she says.

I kneel on the bed so it's less awkward.

"*Thomas?*"

"Yeah?" I say.

"This just got super weird super fast."

"Oh," I say, looking at the two empty champagne glasses on each of our bedside tables.

"I'm gonna go," she says, and turns so her legs emerge from under the blanket.

"It's fine, now," I say, as her feet touch the floor. She reaches down for her clothing, and lays it on the bed next to her. "I don't think she'll come back."

"I don't think that qualifies as fine," she says as she checks her phone. Then she looks at me. "Do you?"

As I look down, Carly rises up. She clasps her bra behind her back with impressive ease. Once her skirt's back on, and she's buttoned her blouse, she pulls on her jacket. Then her phone screen goes bright.

"My Uber's here," she says and walks around the bed toward the exit. She stops a few feet away from where I sit slump-shouldered, wearing only boxer shorts. I breathe in and force my shoulders back.

"So, this finished strong," she says, and points to herself, then me, then herself with a few flicks of her index finger. When I don't answer, she says, "Cool." Then heads toward the door.

After I hear the handle turn, hear the door open, I stand and tell her, "Wait."

But Carly's gone. The momentum of the door spring brings it closer to be closed. Closer, closer, and then *click*.

TWENTY-ONE

WITH CARLY HOURS GONE, it's a call from my father that wakes me up.

"Hello?" I ask as I turn over to check the time. The crinkle of hotel pillows gobbles up the opening of my father telling me, "...is here with your mother."

"Who is?" I ask.

"Sarah," he repeats. I sit up, sparked awake.

"No," I say, bracing.

"Yes," Dad says, which looses in me a whorl of panic. Without me home, Sarah is able to tell them—without nuance, without proper shading—how hard she tried to get me to go home. They won't understand that I wanted to be the good son, but couldn't be. They'll only know what I have been: a coward. "Now will you please just come home?"

I stare at the far wall with great, unblinking concentration and tell him, "With her there, we both know I have to."

It's only 9:21 a.m.

TWENTY-TWO

AT EXACTLY 10:00 A.M., I get a call from EveryOther Films.
"Thomas Mullen?" a cheery male voice asks.

"Yes?" I say, as I zip my luggage, give the room a final check.

"Please hold for Carly Doherty."

While on hold, I pull my nearly forgotten phone charger from an outlet at the base of the bedside lamp.

"Thomas," Carly says, affable. "First, I just want to make sure we're..."

"Something's come up," I say.

"Okay?" she says, lightly annoyed, and waits.

I wait, too.

"Thomas?"

"Yeah?"

"Is everything okay?"

"Something's come up."

"You said." Already, she's lost patience.

I unzip my bag, stuff the phone charger inside.

"Can you tell me where?" Carly asks.

"Where?"

"Where we met."

"I don't know," I say with force, and exhale into the phone.

"Fine," she says.

I watch the digital clock turn to 10:01 a.m. and, right when it does, there's a call on my other line.

"I have another call," I say.

"Thomas, wait. I'm calling because of EO. Your agent hasn't been in touch."

"Just one sec."

"My bosses are pushing to finalize a..."

I click over to the other line and say hello.

"Hey, Thomas, it's Mimi from Anarchy Productions. Sam Gerrard would like to speak to you right away."

"Something's come up."

"Let me just transfer you to Sam," Mimi says. "Hold one sec."

There's a crackle of static and I click over to Carly. "I have to call you back," I say.

"*Thomas,*" she says.

"I said..." I start, my voice breaking.

"I know. '*Something's come up.*'"

"Yes," I say, then I click back over to talk to Sam. After two purring phone rings, he says, "All right, Tommy!"

"I can't right now," I say.

"Is your agent having a giraffe? It's radio silence!"

A broken record, I'm about to crack when I say, "Something's come up."

"But we're talking offer over here, mate. Elvis! Brilliant fuckin' Elvis."

"He'll be in touch," I say.

"Tell him to get his skates on, the plank!"

Off the phone, overwhelmed, I text Ryan, **Your agent isn't calling anyone back!**

My phone immediately rings, a call from Ryan. "It's all part of Peter's plan, but I'm on it. Just focus on getting home safe."

"But people keep calling!" I shout, in a state of near panic.

"I said I'll sort it," he says, severe. Which tells me I've fractured something precious between us.

"Okay," I say.

"Did you get my voicemail?"

"I didn't," I say. "I'll check now." But once I'm off the phone, I don't.

◆◆◆

IN MY RENTAL CAR, nearly at LAX, my phone rings and the area code's **646**. I think: something's come up. I answer, but don't speak.

"I'm sorry to call again, but EO *still* hasn't heard from your agent," Carly's voice says. She speaks slowly, full of calm. "You know my feelings about it, but they're going to hound me to call you until they get an answer."

"Call Ryan," I say.

"Will he actually answer me, since you won't?"

"I have to get home," I say. "My mother's going to die."

TWENTY-THREE

A T LAX, I BOARD a direct to STL. Once I'm buckled in, I text Ryan to tell him I'm on the plane home.

Finally, he writes back. **And I'm so sorry. So is Elsa.**

Jesus. *Elsa.* Who I would like to never see again.

I snap my phone shut and see the closed envelope on my screen, a signal that Ryan's voicemail is still waiting for me. But the effort to dial in feels too exhausting. *Later,* I tell myself, and slip the phone into my pocket. Then lean my head back and close my eyes.

❖❖❖

MIDFLIGHT, I GASP AWAKE in a panic. A rocket shot of certainty blasts through me, so rich I feel it in my teeth: my mother has passed away.

I press my heels into the plane's thin carpet and whisper, "No, no, no."

The man to my left thinks I'm talking to him. I shake my head only a little, then close my eyes. Clamp my hands on the armrests and push back into the seat, trying to catch my breath. Lean my head back and expose my hard-swallowing throat.

My mother, who asked me, "How would you do it? I'm thinking pills."

My mother who said over the phone, "I can't do this without seeing you one last time."

Great, Mom! I thought. *Let's make a weekend of it!*

My mother, who said, "Come home, Thomas. I'm dying. Please give me this."

And I gave her nothing, except a name. *Sarah.* To make her feel like, *He'll be okay. He'll be looked after once I'm gone.*

But then she asked, "What's she like?"

I told her, "Mom, please. I can't do this, Mom. Mom, I love you, but, Mom, Mom, Mom," I said.

And she said, "Okay, Thomas. But before it gets too bad, I want to die."

I raise the shade and rest my elbow on my knee, my chin on my fist, and I watch the outside for some image of my mother. I stay frozen that way, watching. But all I see is a blanket of darkening gray wool below the wing that goes infinitely on and on and on into the sunless, dimming forever.

TWENTY-FOUR

I USE MY NEAR-MAXED credit card to rent a car at STL, and in a fog I drive the speed limit from this bustling middle of nowhere toward the middle of nowhere else. This past I've abandoned. Where Sarah now waits.

I park in my parents' driveway, the same as when I was last home, as if no time's passed. As I walk toward their front door, alongside Dad's always-perfect lawn, an invisible fist squeezes inside my chest, making it hard to breathe. When I step onto the porch, I twist the doorknob. Of course it's locked, so I knock.

When the door opens, Elsa Morris is the one who answers. Her shoes are off and she's wearing lime- and lemon-colored striped socks.

"What?" I finally say, so confused, and tilt my head like a dog intently listening. Half questions speed to the tip of my tongue: Isn't this? How are you? Why is?

Elsa's eyes and the tip of her nose go red. She looks down and whispers, "I'm so sorry."

"But what are *you* doing here?" I snap.

"I'm really, very sorry," she says.

My knees turn to licorice. My throat fills with gravel. Elsa's tone confirms my mother's raindrop of cancer became a puddle became her entire lung, and now she's dead.

Dizzied, I step inside, and ask Elsa, "Where's Sarah?" My ears are clogged from the flight. My voice shotguns around inside my head.

Behind me, Elsa says, "Thomas."

"*Where is she?*" I ask, out of patience with this interfering random. All I want right now is to tell Sarah she was right all along, that I should have come home much, much sooner.

"Sarah?" I say, weakly into the foyer of my parents' home. I feel like maybe I'm hyperventilating. Like maybe I'm on the edge of collapse.

Elsa grabs my arm, insistent. "*Thomas.*"

I jerk my arm away hard and look at her with violence in my eyes. "*Don't.*"

Elsa backs away, looking afraid.

I turn and step forward. Louder now, I say down the hallway, "Sarah?"

"Oh, no," Elsa says behind me. "You didn't listen to Ryan's voicemail."

My father appears from the direction of the dining room, carrying the same go-to coffee mug he's used for ages: *World's Okayest Husband.* The one Mom gave him, way before her asteroid of cancer grew into a meteor that's now grown into her entire lung.

"Sherlock," he says with a pursed smile, happy I'm home. He motions behind me with the hand holding the mug. "You need glasses?"

I turn but it's only Elsa behind me. Her cheeks flushed with red.

I turn back to Dad with a blank expression. He gives me his look that says, *Then I can't help you.*

My lungs spread open to inhale more hysterical air so I can shout for Sarah one hysterical time, when Elsa gently touches my arm. "I know coming here is hard," she says. "But it's okay. I'm right here. Me. *Sarah.*"

The air pushes out of me in a huffed torrent. I turn to Elsa, who makes an effort not to withdraw. Quiet and fierce, I say to her, "What the *fuck?*"

"Language, please," my father says.

"I said I was sorry," Elsa says.

Then behind me, my mother's wounded, songbird voice asks, *"Thomas?"*

"Mom?" I whimper, as tears fill my eyes.

She materializes in the doorway. Resurrected, standing next to my father.

"My little Pop-Tart," she says.

I wipe my eyes clean, in case she's real. "Mom?" I say.

"In the flesh," my father says.

I take a long look at her. "Oh, no," I whisper, confronted by the truth of her cancer's progress. This is what I couldn't bear to see. My mother a skeleton draped in loose skin.

"My baby," my mother says coming to me. "My beautiful boy."

Everything inside me cracks open.

"I'm sorry," I say, trying to catch my breath. At first, my feet won't move. I nearly trip when I take a step toward her. "Mama, I'm so sorry."

I wrap my arms around her. She's no more than a butterfly.

"I'd cry, I'm so happy," she says. "But my tear ducts are blocked." She giggles while she holds me. "Oh, finally," she says.

An *mmm* sound eases from the back of her throat, she's so pleased.

TWENTY-FIVE

SOON AFTER MY ARRIVAL, while I hold my mother's hand, she tells us, "I need to head upstairs for a LLD."

"LLD?" Elsa asks.

"A little lie down," Mom says with a wink. "I don't feel worth a shit."

I don't want to be away from her, not for a second, so I help her up the stairs and into my parents' bed.

"Do you need a blanket or water?" I ask, once she's lying down. "I can fluff your pillow."

With her eyes closed, she shakes her head. "Don't fuss," she says, and falls right to sleep. I watch her breathe in pained, shallow gulps.

Minutes later, I head downstairs to overhear Elsa—the phone returner, the unwelcome—fielding questions from my father in the living room.

"Sarah, where'd you grow up?" he asks.

"Sad sack Sacramento."

Dad laughs. "Oh, it can't be that bad."

"I think it might be."

When I enter the room, Dad asks if Mom's okay. I tell him, "She fell asleep like *that*."

"She does that now," he says, and takes notice when I sit in Mom's armchair, instead of on the couch next to Elsa-as-Sarah. "Does she bite?" Dad asks me.

"Once in a while," Elsa says, and glances at me, then looks down.

"And your parents," Dad starts. "What do they do?"

"My father's an industrial engineer," Elsa says, as she creates an all-new Sarah. A Sarah I've never met. "And Mom helps organize democratic political campaigns."

"And now you work caring for children?"

"Adults, actually. I teach art therapy to people who have experienced trauma."

❖❖❖

SOON ENOUGH, ELSA RISES and asks my father if he'd like more tea. He shakes his head and says no thanks.

"I would," I say. "I'll help you make it."

Elsa picks up my father's empty mug and her own, then I follow her into the kitchen. Once we're out of my father's sightline, her head goes down and she beelines to the sink. She rinses the mugs, and once the faucet's off she turns and I say quietly, so my dad can't hear, "You being here is insane."

"Look, I really am very sorry. But your father asked me to come."

"Great!" I say, all sarcastic.

"He kept calling me Sarah."

"And why not fly two thousand miles under false pretenses to continue a batshit lie?"

Elsa's brow clouds. She crosses her arms tight across her chest. "We didn't know how much longer she had left."

"*We!*" I say. "Holy shit."

"Your mother's so happy you're here," she says.

"Well, yeah, of course she's happy, because now she gets to die."

Elsa squeezes herself even tighter with her arms.

"I'll leave," she says. "I'll pack up now and go."

I laugh. "And how's that going to look?" I say. Then I get mean. "Now you're here until the bitter end."

The oven timer *beep-beep-beeps*. Elsa makes a move, but I take a long stride toward the oven so she stops.

"I put a pizza in," she says. I'm about to chastise her for making herself at home, but I soften when she says, "So none of us forget to eat."

I press the timer off, and without opening the oven door all the way I slide a cookie sheet between the crust and the rack. The back of my left wrist touches the inside of the oven door and *sizzles*. Quick like a gasp, I say, "Fuck!" and let go of the cookie sheet with a clang.

"You okay?" Elsa asks.

"Yeah," I say, looking at my wrist, waiting for the pain.

"Everything all right?" Dad asks, and makes his way in from the living room.

"Yes," I say. "Everything is A-plus-plus."

"I told her we could order Imo's," Dad says. "But as long as you still have your hand, I guess this'll do."

❖❖❖

It's around dusk when Mom slowly descends the stairs. I meet her at the bottom, and she gives me two kisses on my right cheek. Then she shuffles into the living room, takes Elsa by the wrists, and looks her in the eye. "I'm so glad you're here," she says.

"Me, too," Elsa says followed by a smile that collapses as soon as she sees me.

Mom eases onto the couch and, when she's settled, she pats the cushion next to her, an invitation. I sit as close to her as I can without cramping.

Dad comes in with a mug of chamomile and sets it on the coffee table in front of Mom.

"Now?" Mom asks him, as Dad sits.

"Now, what?" I ask her.

"Now, sure," Dad says.

Mom does a little wriggle next to me to straighten up, and Dad uncrosses his legs, breathes in deep, then lets out a smooth, concentrated exhale. Both clear signals that we're about to embark on something major.

Which I am not ready for, and it fills me with panic.

"Mom?" I say, and I sit up, too.

She hears the alarm in my voice and says, "It's okay."

"It's not," I say.

"What's up?" Elsa says, with an expression of clear unease.

"Your mother just wants to talk," Dad says.

I push my hands into the couch cushions, press my heels into the carpet, an attempt to slow time, to stop it.

"I told you about a year ago that I couldn't do this without seeing you again," Mom says.

"Mom, please," I say, and now I can't catch my breath.

"Sweetheart," Mom says, and puts her hand on my leg, which calms me. Then she turns to me and takes my face in her hands and kisses me on the cheek. "My sweet, sweet Thomas."

I nod, and she takes her hands away.

"I'm not going anywhere," she says. "Not tonight. I just want to tell you."

"Tell me what?"

"Everything."

I look at Dad for a clue, but he's just nodding at me with a pleasant expression. Then I turn to Mom. "I don't know what that means."

"You're about to," Dad says.

I look down to check in. My breathing's mellowed, and my hands have stopped shaking.

"Okay," I say. "Okay."

Then I look up and see Elsa fidgeting.

"*Wait*," I say. "Sarah doesn't need to hear all this."

Elsa takes the cue, and stands abruptly. "Yeah, I'll just go upstairs."

"Sit," Mom says to her. "Please."

"I can't," Elsa says and turns like she's going to go, but then stops. Her eyes flash my way, but all I can offer is a blank expression. But it's my mother's face, my mother's nod, that withers any inkling of an exit, and Elsa collapses back into her chair.

"I imagine you two share everything, anyway," Mom says. "This saves you from having to repeat it all later."

Then she takes a cleansing breath, and begins.

TWENTY-SIX

THIRTY-NINE YEARS AGO, YOUR mother falls in love with her first love. A man who's twenty-three, older than she is by two years. It's storybook. This man, Carl Mixen, is everything to your mother and she is everything to him. Three months later, they're married.

Carl is so happy, and so is your mother.

This is your mother, and you aren't born yet.

Three weeks later, a call from the hospital: Carl's been in a car accident. No one's hurt. No one's dead. But something in his brain has balloon burst and half of him is stripped down to body without movement. Your mother goes to the hospital where the doctor tells her, "He should have never married, his brain the way it is. Aneurysms." The word, frightening alien speak.

At night, in the dark, your mother holds Carl in her arms and tells him how much she loves him. "I'm here," she says. "I'm right here."

Carl's mouth is never a full smile; still he glows because of his good luck. This is how the man your mother loves thinks of himself: Lucky. His beatific life, ending in three, two, one aneurysms.

Fast forward three years to Carl's next-to-final aneurysm. Your mother saying: "Don't go, please. Stay with me. You're all

I have." Carl is crippled movement. He is slurred speech. *I'm here,* he mouths. *I'm right here.*

Fast-forward four months to your sleeping mother snapping awake. It's 6:00 a.m. She whispers Carl's name into the empty room. She moves through their house silent and finds Carl, motionless in the hallway. This is your mother's life. Her first love, an empty body. Her first love, now gone.

Two years pass. Your mother is slow-moving with a wounded heart. She works as a secretary and a receptionist. She makes ends meet.

Then, with no fireworks or sense of fate, she meets a man named Martin Arnold who is kind enough, who is loving enough, who is enough enough.

Martin and your mother marry. With Martin, your mother is soon pregnant. She misses Carl. But here, a new life brewing. Nine months and this new child—Joshua—is born.

Time passes, and there is another child on the way. We'll call this child Thomas. We'll call this child you.

It is January. You are still in the womb. Your family inside a sedan. The roads are slick and the tires find a patch of black ice. The car glides and sways and the back end collides with a truck with one, two, three, eighteen wheels.

A miracle, then: everyone survives. Your mother, your father, Joshua, and in-the-womb you. But. Joshua's head is smashed so badly he can only breathe while on a machine. The doctors say lots of things, but they can be summed up by: *It's only a matter of time.*

Your mother, this poor woman. Your mother's lone living son is counting down. His arms twisted sticks. Legs purple and knotted. Tick tock.

This is your mother's life, what's left of it.

Then comes you. A post-traumatic stress birth. A premature breach birth. Followed by so much blood. Concerns that neither you nor she will make it. Emergency surgery, then her tubes tied. The last child your mother will ever have. Thomas.

Six days after you're born, Joshua, your brother, passes.

This is how your mother lived another life that didn't include you. This is what she tells you, your mother, while your father and Elsa look on silent.

This is your mother telling you secrets she's never told you before. This is why she stayed alive while you were too afraid to let her die.

You put your arms around your mother so tight it feels like she's crumbling. Tomorrow, after an early dinner, now that you're home and she has told you what there is to tell, you will help her die.

So here you are, repeating the same two words—I'm sorry, I'm sorry, I'm sorry—as you're hugging her, and she is holding you. To counter your two words, she says two words of her own. Over and over. "I know," she says. "I know. I know. I *know*."

TWENTY-SEVEN

A FTER MOM'S TURNED IN and Elsa's upstairs in the queen bed I slept in until I was eighteen, Dad and I sit in the living room's low light.

"You okay?" Dad asks.

"Heartbroken," I say. "Shell-shocked." He nods and scratches his nose with a knuckle.

"What your mother told you," he says. "I want you to know we weren't trying to hide anything from you."

"I think I get it," I say quietly, because I think I do.

Plus, so much is clear, now. The quiet in the house when I was young. January's month-long candlelight vigils. A reluctance to drive in inclement weather. Full hugs from my mother that would go on so long. And my father's trancelike silences that I'd feel guilty to interrupt, though every time I did his warmth was immediate.

"We wanted to protect you," Dad says. "Losing your brother..." He pauses, and his eyes momentarily close while his hands fold together over his belly, as if in prayer. He forces an exhale through his nose. "I don't talk about it. For years we talked through it, but now it's something between us that's not spoken. I haven't said his name in twenty years."

"I wish I'd met him," I say.

"Oh, me, too."

Joshua, my brother who I'll never know. I imagine him full-grown, someone I could meet, now that I know he exists. But he never saw his fifth birthday; he's been dead thirty-three years.

"It's late," Dad says, without a glance at his watch, or turning to see the clock on the wall behind him. "Or it's getting there." He stands and looks at Mom's tea mug, alone on the table.

"I'll clean up," I say.

"Don't," he says, eyes still on the mug. "And I mean that. Leave it, please."

I tell him I will, then I tell him goodnight.

"Tomorrow is a big day," he says. "A very, very big day."

❖❖❖

WHEN I ENTER MY bedroom, Elsa's in the en suite, so I scratch around the burn on my wrist that stings like an itch. I turn it toward the light to see the blotch of shiny skin and the curl of a few toasted hairs.

A fire ignites in me when Elsa comes out of the bathroom, quiet, and says, "Let me see."

"*No,*" I say, spiteful. Then I sit on the bed I'm forced to share with a total stranger so my mother can continue to make believe she's Sarah.

"I'm sorry, okay? I'm really, *really* sorry," Elsa says and stops at the foot of the bed. "I know my being here is crazy, and that I'm in the way, but I swear I came here because I was trying to help." She pushes her fingertips into her hair. "I mean I am at your freakin' *parents'* house, in the suburbs of *St. Louis,*" she says. Her arms flop to her sides. "What the *fuck* am I doing?"

"I don't know," I fire back, unforgiving. "I seriously have no idea."

Elsa walks to her side of the bed, and turns her back to me. "This is just way too much, and I am in way too deep."

"Why did you come?"

"I guess because your mother sounded lost on the phone," Elsa says, and crosses her arms. "She was dying, and I wanted to give her comfort."

I don't move. I just stare at her.

"And...and probably because this whole thing gained momentum out of nowhere." She turns away from me, then back. "Before I knew it, it was a runaway thing I couldn't get off."

"But you. Why did *you* come?"

"Because I'm a little Goody Two-shoes who's always believed if the moment presented itself, I could save the day."

"Bullshit."

"It's not," she says, and turns to me.

"But you are getting warmer," I say, because there's more, something she doesn't want to say. "But who pretends to be someone else and fly two thousand miles? That's specific to you, and it's not sane."

"Sane? Who sits by while their dying mother fades to nothing?" Elsa says and her eyes go wet. "She's in so much pain—she's *been* in so much pain. She begged you to come home, and you waited and waited, for what?"

She wipes under both her eyes with a swipe of her index finger.

"The real reason, the really real reason, is I'm here because you didn't have the guts to come. And someone had to."

"I'm here," I say, the thinnest defense. But I know she's right.

Then the sound of her cell phone ringing, a low series of beeps, from downstairs.

"Somebody's phone," my father says from down the hall.

Elsa exhales, clumsily opens the door, and leaves it open after she exits. I hear her hurried steps down the carpeted stairs, and as she's coming back up, I hear her voice downshift into inaudible whisper.

When she's back in my room, she closes the door and hands me her phone.

"Who is it?" I ask.

Drained, she jabs the phone at me like, *Just take it.*

I answer with an unsure hello.

"Why is your phone going straight to voicemail?" Ryan asks.

"I guess it died?"

"Well, charge it."

"How did you know Elsa was here?" I ask him.

"What do you mean?" he says. "I said on your voicemail she was on her way." The voicemail I never got around to checking.

"And how did you know she was coming here?" I ask as I look up at Elsa, who's pacing back and forth with her arms crossed, chewing at the tip of her right thumb.

"Because we talk every day?"

"What?"

"What 'what'?" Ryan says.

I suddenly feel like I'm part of a murder mystery, and this is the moment I realize that every person I see on stage, everyone *involved*, is somehow—until now, unbeknownst to me—connected.

"Is everything okay?" Ryan asks me.

"Everything's fucking brilliant," I tell him. "My mom's been decimated by my inaction, and a total stranger, pretending to be the love of my life, just tore into me."

"You're home," he says, trying to soothe me.

"Great," I breathe out, feeling defeated.

"You can't see it now, but it is great."

"Is it?" I ask. "Because tomorrow I get to see my mom again. Then after dinner, I *never* get to see her again."

TWENTY-EIGHT

AFTER A FRESH-FRUIT BREAKFAST, Mom and I sit alone on the couch, a blanket over her legs. A photo album on her lap.

"Here he is when he was two," she says, and points to a picture of Joshua. He's standing in snow up to his ankles, a branch in his right hand and a wool cap over his ears. I search for signs that he looks like me. But he looks like any child, really. Unformed and sweet.

My mother runs her thumb over the picture. I can feel her remembering.

When the spell breaks, I ask her, "Where were these pictures when I was young?"

"We didn't want to confuse you," she says. "So once you started walking, we kept the pictures deep in drawers and put his clothing in boxes in the attic."

"You hid them away?" I ask. "And not just from me, but from yourselves."

"That's not how it was," Mom says. "Memories of him were everywhere. He was never hidden from us. Year after year, your father and I would talk about going up to the attic and paring his things down to those essential, heart-aching items we couldn't let go. But we never did throw anything away. Why put ourselves through having to choose? Your father can show you, if you want. But it always takes him a day to recover. As for the pictures, we looked at them when we could stand it. When you were in bed, or at school."

"I remember the candles," I say.

"We still do it. All of January," she says. "We keep a town full of candlemakers in business."

When I was young I'd asked why they lit candles, and my parents told me the same thing every year: "To remember those we've lost." I never asked for specifics, and since all of my grandparents had passed before I was born, I assumed the candles were for them.

"You could have told me," I say.

"Maybe," she says. "But it feels like there was no right answer."

All this helps me connect the dots between my parents' ongoing mourning and my own reservations about speaking up or speaking out. I was a quiet, careful child who learned to step gently in the world. I hadn't thought of it for years, but now I remember going to bed at night in grade school, for months straight, feeling like the planet itself would unravel if either of my parents were to die.

"I guess we felt like we didn't want your life tied to that night," Mom says. "After the accident, the doctors said you were in perfect health. But it was hard to believe in anything when Joshua was on life support. You came a month early, and six days after that, Joshua slipped away. I remember holding you that night. Our sweet little pea who'd come early, in a hurry to save us."

My mother puts her hand on my knee and holds it there. Warmth spreads all through my leg. I feel ashamed for all the times she was made to suffer while I denied her, over and over, by not coming home these past years. And upset that I didn't know about Joshua decades ago.

"I nearly missed all this," I say.

"But you didn't," she says, and gently squeezes my leg. With her free hand, she turns backward through the plastic pages, some that need to be pried apart. "And we cannot allow ourselves to live a life of what-ifs."

But don't I? Every day. Wondering what-if, with Sarah.

"Oh, here," she says at the sight of two pictures of a man, on Christmas morning. In one, he's sitting with his back to an ornamented tree. In another, he's stuffing a fistful of wrapping paper in his mouth.

"Is that him?" I ask.

"That's Carl," she says.

"He looks nice."

"He was every single kindness," she says. "I remember taking these pictures. I remember that morning. I was six weeks pregnant with Helen."

"Helen?" I ask. My first thought is: please, *please*, don't let my mother have suffered the death of another of her children.

She nods, and puts her thumb on the picture, over her stomach.

"Six weeks after this was taken—I don't know if it was fatigue, or just bad luck—there was a crippling sting, then a shriek of blood. I miscarried, and Helen was gone."

Mom looks at me, her lips pressed tight together. She nods and says, "I cried and cried, and Carl never wavered. 'I'm here,' he said. 'I'm here. I'm right here.' I was so young then. I still believed the world was limitless. That God had gifted the three of us forever."

My mother's weak arms struggle to lift the heavy album to her face. She kisses the picture of Carl with wrapping paper in his mouth, then gives another kiss to her belly. She flips forward and finds Joshua standing in the snow, and kisses that one, too. Then closes the album.

"I don't want to leave you, or your father, who has been perfect in the face of all storms," my mother says to me, her voice swelling so she has to swallow. "But it gives me so much relief that I'll see them all very soon." Mom stares down at the closed album, then leans forward for her half-filled mug of chamomile. She can't reach, so I hand her the cup. She takes the smallest sip. "And if it doesn't work that way, then I guess I'll just die," she says. "But at least I get to take them with me."

TWENTY-NINE

IN THE GROCERY STORE near my parents' house, my father and
I shop for Mom's Last Supper. We're standing mid-aisle for
minutes, my father staring at all of the macaroni and cheese
options, until I ask, "Dad? You okay?"

"Is this the good one?" he asks, and grabs a no-flash box
labeled with the word "organic," instead of holding up the
noisier option that promises to pack a Bigger! Cheeeeesier!
Wallop Than Ever Before!

"I'm sure it's fine," I say.

"You used to love spirals," he says, like everything is far
away. "You eat those anymore?"

"Dad, you sure you're okay?"

He holds the organic box of mac and cheese in both hands
and tells me, "I just want to get this right."

My father drops the box in the cart, then walks away. The
cart between us, I watch him move, a slight sway to his steps,
the look of a lost child.

I grip the shopping cart handle like I'm revving it, and
feel a gentle sting at the back of my left wrist. I see the burn
from yesterday, when I pulled the frozen pizza from the oven
without care. I study the oven's mark. This brown-purple V.

This oversize sear freckle. This commemorative stamp of my mother's passing. I hope it stays. I hope it scars.

I push the cart an aisle over, where my father studies the shelves for All-New Flavor Crystals! and Twice the Taste, HALF the Price!

"This is all made by the same people," he says, waving at the filled shelves. "And it's all crap. But we buy it all the same. Let's grab some fresh fish, then double back for the rest."

My father walks away, toward the back of the store, and I follow.

"Your mother and I agree that Sarah is a very good egg," he says to me. "And I know it does your mother a world of good to know that once she's gone, you won't be alone."

And there's something in his tone that's a tell: Dad's figured out that Sarah isn't really Sarah. That Elsa's a fill-in, playing make-believe.

We arrive at the seafood counter, where we gaze through arched, clear windows at an assortment of headless fish positioned on half-inch-wide nuggets of white ice.

A stout woman trudges over, white smock, white hat, hands covered in cheap, ill-fitting, translucent gloves. Her lips look more purple than pink. "What can I help you with?" she says.

"Tilapia was a symbol of rebirth in Egyptian art," my father tells her. "So let's go with that. Enough for four."

The woman nods, then reaches down and opens the door to the fish without dipping her head below counter level. I watch her hand feel around before it locks on to two filets. She backs up and slaps them onto a wide rectangle of yellow paper before she goes back in for two more.

"Your mother's been wanting to die for a long time," he tells me.

"Excuse me?" the woman behind the counter says.

"His mother," my father says, and gestures to me. I hold my breath, afraid he'll repeat what he's just told me. Afraid someone else will know. "We're making her dinner."

I exhale, trying to make zero noise.

"Growing up, I showed you too good of an example of how to be removed," Dad says. "Or at least distant. Which is a useless shame. But you lucked out. There's way more of your mother in you than me. Which is why I knew you'd come home."

I look down. I took so long. I took too long.

"Don't beat yourself up, though I know you will," he says. "But understand that every day you stayed away was another day with her."

The woman behind the counter has wrapped, taped, and price-tagged the fish. She watches, intently. "Sir," she says, when she decides my father is finished.

Dad faces her, and she slides the package toward him. He takes it and looks at the price tag, like there's some secret hidden in the numbers. She turns her attention onto me, so I force a smile in her direction. Satisfied, she looks at my father, who turns and heads down the nearest aisle, the package of fish in his hands. I don't immediately go. I turn my back and look the length of the counter at the bright fluorescent lights maxing out every color: the orange-pink salmon, the tuna's gel-like deep red, the snowy silver whitefish. I breathe in the congesting sea scent and consider the impact of my twofold past. Raised as an only child, but really I'm the second of two children. Wait, no. There's Helen. By Mom's count, I'm the last of three.

I push the cart toward Dad. He's eyeballing spaghetti sauce injected with More Flavor Than EVER! that has The Freshest Ingredients You'll Find Anywhere!

"Dad?" I say when I get close. "Dad?"

He turns with a tired, "Huh?"

"Why the name Helen?"

"Helen?" His brow creases. The rows of red sauce are so ruby and rich and savory and fantastic-tasting that lined up like this, they look absolutely bland.

"*Hel*en," I say, enforcing her name's first syllable, making it obvious that this is his wife's miscarried daughter. "Is it a family name?"

"I don't know how you mean," he says. But what he means is he doesn't know whom I mean.

"Oh, shit," I say, and take a sudden, distracted interest in the sixty frozen Paul Newman faces smiling at me from spaghetti sauce labels.

"Who's Helen, Thomas?"

"Let's get home," I say, feeling the sudden press of time. Every moment we're away from my mother, we'll never get back—the minutes of her life quickly dwindling.

"We should have sent Sarah," I say, buying into the lie for my mother's sake. "Why are we even here, really? We need to *go*."

I start to wheel the cart toward the store's front, and my father grabs my shoulder hard.

"Tell me," he says.

"You need to ask Mom," I say, and he looks at me with such rich sadness. "It's fine, Dad. Everything is fine. I just really want to be home with Mom, now."

I look at my father who gazes into the cart, empty save for this dinner's necessities and packaging flooded with false, exclamatory promises. Life as he's lived it, for so long, is hours from vanishing.

I push the cart toward the front of the store, and Dad follows. As we near the end of the aisle, the store opens wide. Beyond the stretch of registers, I see the multiple exits ahead. My mother dies if I go home. But if I leave town now, maybe I save her. If I rush out of one of those doors, maybe she recovers and goes right on living. All I have to do is run. Run and run and never stop running.

THIRTY

M Y MOTHER'S LAST SUPPER in full swing, Mom talks freely and cheerily about her past, including living in Germany, where her father was stationed. I listen with fascinated interest as she tells Elsa, "I was sixteen and *no way* would my father let me drive."

I try to gauge my father's reaction, but he's smiling. Even though tomorrow, he's a widow.

"Back then he'd be gone a month at a time," my mother says. "And once, my mother went back to America without me to take care of her own mother, who was ill. So I was on my own. When Daddy left, he took the car keys, so I was held hostage in Frankfurt. Which, I have to say, is no great shakes at any age."

I add up my mother's children on my fingers. My thumb is Joshua. I name my pinkie Helen. My index finger is me.

My mom says to me, "The Thomas *you* were named after was my cousin, who was in the Army." Then to everyone: "Tommy Fox and his wife were stationed in Heidelberg. Only sixty-five miles away, but I had no way to get to them. Until a friend of mine on base, a *sympathizer*, showed me what I could do with two hairpins."

I want to know what Elsa's face is doing, what my father's expression is, but my mother holds me with her sunken eyes.

"So a week after my father had gone, I went out to the car, took those two hairpins and hot-wired the son of a bitch!"

We all laugh along with my mother, a celebration of her boldness, her joyful retelling. But her excitement turns into stalled breath followed by coughing. We all go quiet while she brings her clenched fist to her throat and forces a swallow. After a resigned moan, I'm thinking: there won't need to be a pill overdose. No point of a lethal injection. Things will end soon enough for her all on their own.

"After that," Mom continues quietly, "I headed to Heidelberg."

I look at my mother, her body a failing echo, her skin inked with pain. If this is her Last Supper, then we are the apostles. I look around the table. First, to my father, silent and drawn. Then Elsa, all forced smiles and desperation. When I use the back of a spoon to see my warped reflection, I think: *I refused to come home, so that's one betrayal. Two is I haven't told my mother the truth about Sarah. Is there a third?*

Everyone's plate but my mother's is filled with broiled tilapia, buttery mashed potatoes, and string beans drizzled with soy sauce. A half hour before dinner, her arm wrapped into my arm, my mother said to me in confidence, "Don't give me too much, I don't want to barf all over the table." Her small portion of fish, small enough to disappear with one big fork scoop.

"But on the way to Heidelberg I started getting worried I'd be pulled over," Mom says. "So I pulled off in Darmstadt and found the German equivalent of the DMV, so I could get my driver's license."

I look at my father and think: *Not dodging a steamrolling semi is one betrayal. Being a quiet ghost is two. For him, is there a three?*

"So I'm driving with this instructor in the stolen car, whipping right through the test," my mother says. "I'm on the right side of the road—in Germany you're on the right side, same as America. But then I stall the car while parallel parking—the damn thing was a stick shift. I tried to restart it, but of course there's no key! I nearly shit."

My mother and her grand theft auto has Elsa enthralled. For Elsa I think: *The first betrayal is coming here. Posing as Sarah is two. What's three?*

"So right in front of the driving instructor I reach down, fiddle with the hairpins. The car started right up. And if you can believe it, he passed me!" Elsa spurts a laugh of disbelief. "I couldn't believe it, either."

My mother, smiling, scoops up the last of her fish, guides it into her mouth, and chews.

I look around the table and think: *What is the third betrayal?*

I look at my mother and think: *Hiding your past for my entire life is one. Asking your child and husband to kill you is two. But three?*

My mother chews with weak teeth, a weak jaw, her entire body a fraction of a fraction of a fraction. The cancer has stretched out its arms and legs. It's in her bones and stomach. It's in her liver and what's left of her uterus. It crowds her lungs.

I try a bite of the fish. It's gummy and cool.

My mother notices that I've taken a bite, and that no one else has in too long. "Good, Thomas," she says and pats my wrist, then holds on to it. The faltering control of her mouth works into a smile. "Thank you."

Followed by the brief, fractured song of cutlery on plates as we, nearly in unison, all take a bite.

My mother's still-flickering eyes look over at Elsa, who she thinks is Sarah. Elsa's pushing a green bean with the tines of her fork when my father asks, "Rosemary, who's Helen?"

"Oh, Marty."

"Don't 'Oh, Marty' me," my father says.

"Like it matters at this point. But she was my daughter. Or would have been. But I miscarried. It happened a very long time ago."

"Why didn't you ever tell me?" Dad says, visibly hurt.

"I don't know," my mother says. "Maybe she was only mine."

"You could have told me."

"I know."

My father looks down at his plate for only a moment.

"Look at me, Marty. Please."

Their eyes have already met. His are darkened and teary. Hers are jaundiced and at peace. What she wants him to remember is context. And now we've all got it. *Look at me.* There's no room or need for fault. Not anymore. Now her body is a framework of broken-down parts eager to expire that should have been given relief long ago.

In this way, near the end of my mother's final dinner, the third betrayal is revealed to me. I look around the table at my mother, my father, at Elsa. But there is no hope of shifting blame to these three, the unassailable. I am the one that did not let my mother die.

The third and final betrayal: it is all mine.

THIRTY-ONE

M Y MOTHER LEADS US up the stairs to her bedroom—
my father, Elsa, then me. Her fragile legs work slowly.
She's in no rush and wants no help.

Three-quarters of the way up, a throat-stripping cough
stops her. She pulls a Kleenex from the pocket of her mauve
terrycloth robe and spits a gurgle of phlegm into it the way she
always has: by licking the Kleenex, moving the mess from her
tongue to paper. I watch the transfer closely. There's no blood.
She balls the Kleenex up and tucks it into her pocket.

"Rosie?" my father says and stops.

"Marty?" my mother says back, only a stair above him.

"Can you not do this, please?" he says quietly.

My mother leans into my father's arms, an embrace.
"I know you don't mean it," she says, her face over his shoulder.
"We both know I have to go."

Dad looks at me, so I'll say something.

I look at my mother's scalp, beneath fragile strands of
drained hair. Her withered outline. This time, I don't argue.
This time, I show mercy.

"What am I supposed to do?" Dad says.

Elsa's uneasy. She looks away from my parents, then turns
and takes a step down the stairs toward me, in a clear attempt
to avoid this premortem melodrama.

"No," I say. I don't let Elsa pass, won't let her escape unscathed from what's soon coming.

To her credit, she doesn't put up a fight. She simply closes her eyes, inhales a deep breath, then turns back in the direction of upstairs, of my embracing parents.

"I made notes for you," Mom says to my father. Which explains why the coffee pot has instructions on a 3x5 note card taped to it:

MAKING COFFEE

- Remove coffee filter.
- Pour in 2 ½ cups of water.
- Put ¾ of a scoop of coffee in a filter.
- Place filter in top of machine.
- Hit red button.
- Wait.
- Drink.

And why the breadbasket has a 3x5 note card taped to it:

TEN DAYS, NO MORE. THEN <u>THROW IT OUT!</u>

"You'll be okay," my mother says. "You all will."

"You don't know that," Dad says.

"We both do," she says.

My father looks at me, helpless. I look back at him with a determined expression that conveys: this is right and it is time to save her life by letting her go. A look that hides the fear and exhaustion I feel inside. There are so few people in the world who love me, and soon there will be one less.

My father swallows, then composes. He turns back to my mother, who quietly says into my father's ear, "Thank you for taking such good care of me." Her eyes are closed, like she's dreaming.

THIRTY-TWO

OUTSIDE THE WINDOW OF my parents' bedroom, the moon is a haze of pale light covered by the thick gloom of charcoal clouds. Down below is our wide, lush yard, cared for by my father. I see movement in the yard's far corner and tilt my head forward. But it's nothing.

Behind me, my father sits in a chair beside my mother, who lies beneath fresh, flannel sheets. He asks her, "Do you need more water?"

I turn to see her shake her head. Seconds ago, she swallowed down pills that her doctor gave her with explicit instructions: "If you take *more than one dose* of this, it would be *lethal.*" Hint, hint.

Elsa's jittery in the doorway, staying put at my request, but her nerves are apparent. She chews at the tip of her index finger while trading her weight from her left foot to her right, then back.

"Thomas," my mother says. She reaches for me from her bed and when I move to her, she tugs at my untucked shirt so I'll lean down. She kisses me near the mouth with dry lips and I kiss her back. Her breathing is weak and shallow.

"Does it hurt?" I ask. I sit on the bed.

"Probably," she says with a smile. She takes my hand. Hers feels like cool paper. "I love you," she says.

"Me, too," I say.

"No, say it. I want to hear."

"I love you, Mama."

She closes her eyes and makes an *mmm* sound.

It's more than I can handle. I pull away from my mother and she lets me go. I don't take my eyes off of her as I go back to the window to suck in a series of deep, calming breaths.

I glance over at Elsa who's pressed her forehead against the doorjamb while holding a Kleenex to her face.

My father holds my mother's elbow in his left hand while his chin rests on his right fist. To look at him, he hasn't slept in weeks.

It's fifteen minutes later when my mother becomes delirious. "Helen?" she says, and none of us understand. *"Helen."*

My father and I realize she's talking to Elsa, so Dad snaps to get her attention. Elsa, the pretender, the interloper, is still in the doorway with her head down. The snap makes her look up.

When she does, my mother lifts her arm and waves Elsa over. "Come closer." Elsa comes closer. "Closer." Elsa stands at the corner at the foot of the bed. "Take care of these two little shits," she says. "Take money from my purse and buy them ice creams."

Elsa nods, her mouth a quivering frown as tears stream down her face.

My mother's energy spikes and she turns to my father with sudden clarity. "When Joshua died, that was the most terrible day," she says as a matter-of-fact while my father holds my mother's hand to his forehead. "Wasn't it?"

"It was," Dad says, nodding.

Then she turns to me and stares. "You're such a beautiful young man. But you do need to get that haircut." An echo of what she'd tell me when I was in my teens and twenties.

"Okay," I say, and my face goes hot.

Next, Mom stares at the ceiling, her eyes glossing. "I'm plum worn out."

For the next silent minutes, we watch her breathe.

To break the roiling of tension, I stand and go to the window, stare out into the blank night.

When I turn to my mom and tell her, "Mom, please, I know you need to go, but it's okay to stay. I'm here for as long as…"

My father holds up his hand, a stop sign. Which cuts me off.

"She's gone," he says.

"What?" I ask, staring at him. I swallow, then follow his eyes as he looks down at my mother, his wife.

"Your mother has passed," he says.

"How?" I say. But of course I know how.

Elsa, at the foot of the bed, makes a choking sound. Then my father starts crying. Somehow, I don't. When Elsa turns quick toward the door and takes a step to exit, my father snaps again, which stops her mid-step. He says to her, "No. Not yet."

Elsa acquiesces, wiping her eyes. Then follows with a pair of wet sniffles.

"I just want to remember," my father says, his hand still on Mom's right elbow.

While I hold my mom's cooling hand, I ask Dad, "Is it okay?"

After a while he says, "I guess so." He looks at me while he guesses so. "I think so." He kisses my mother's forehead, then looks down at her, finally, before he decides, "Yes."

THIRTY-THREE

THE NEXT MORNING, I wake from a deep, dreamless sleep to Elsa whispering my name. When I open my eyes, she's kneeling on my bedroom floor, holding her phone out in front of her. I'm flat on my stomach, my cheek on the sheets, a pillow pressed against the top of my head. I don't say a word. Just blink.

"Sorry," she says. "I'm so sorry." Then I remember: my mother's dead. "But it's Ryan."

Last night, my father called the hospital to report what had happened. I watched him closely as he spoke into the phone. Everything decelerated. I became aware of my fingers. The cramped way my feet felt in my shoes. My shoulders were still tensed and started to ache. All actions felt deliberate, my father's slightest facial tics rich with meaning. By the time he'd hung up, maybe ten minutes later, I felt impossibly exhausted. I was upright, but my eyelids started to close. After they'd come to take my mother's body, I was so tired, it became difficult to stand. I got into my bed. I didn't care that I had to share it with Elsa. I'd never felt so tired in my entire life. I closed my eyes, and it was all darkness straight through to Elsa whispering me awake.

"Can you talk?" Elsa asks me, now.

"Debatable," I say, without moving.

"If there's anything I can do," she says.

I turn my head slightly and try to give her a look that says: there's nothing to be done.

"He can call back," she says.

I shake my head, then work my arm out from under the blankets and hold it out, palm down. She puts the phone in my hand, and I grip it loosely. She goes out of the door as I set her phone on my face, and let my free arm dangle over the side of the bed. I breathe into the phone to alert Ryan it's me.

"Thomas?" he asks.

"Mhmm," I grunt, mouth closed.

"How are you feeling?" he asks.

"Depressed."

I hear him take a breath. "I'm sorry you lost your mom," he says.

"Me, too."

"Anarchy and EO submitted official offers for Elvis."

I blink. Then I blink again.

"That doesn't matter now, I know. Just thought you might like some good news."

I take a deep breath and a lung-clearing exhale.

"Do you want to get off the phone?" he asks.

"No," I say. I breathe in, then out, then in. "Yes."

"Then I'll call later," he says. "I just wanted you to know I'm here. Okay?"

I nod. Because of the nod, the phone slides off my face, and onto the floor. I reach down and drag my fingers slowly along the carpet. When I finally find it, I don't check if Ryan's still on the line before I hang up.

Soon after, Elsa knocks on the door. I don't tell her to enter before she pushes it open and peeks in. "Okay if I come in?"

I hold out her phone and she takes it.

"I'm going to leave today," she says. I see her red carry-on that's been wide open since I arrived. It's packed up, standing upright against the wall. "It's time."

❖❖❖

I COME DOWNSTAIRS JUST after 10:00 a.m., and Elsa has, by request, made my father lunch for breakfast—penne pasta topped by a red sauce riddled with tomato chunks and sprinkled with basil.

"Do you want some?" she asks me.

"Okay."

As Elsa prepares a plate for me, I sit across from my father at our kitchen table. His lips pinch together and he nods at me.

I look down and nod right back.

He picks up his fork, digs a tomato chunk loose from the noodles, and takes a bite.

"Any moment now, I expect her to come from behind some door," Dad says, sounding winded. "I woke up earlier and opened every door in the house, just to see. Then I went back through and did it again."

I look and see Elsa's holding my plate, waiting for the right time to bring it to me.

My dad looks straight down into his plate. She takes a step forward, then stops when he says, "Who ever came up with 'grown men don't cry'?"

"Yeah," I say, though something inside me is holding on, holding back.

Elsa steps forward again. This time she puts my plate in front of me.

"That hasn't been true for twenty years," Elsa says, and rubs my father's back. His body starts to shudder, and I watch a single, sizable teardrop fall on top of a concentration of red sauce, creating a crater.

I start breathing heavy and lean back in my chair.

"Please don't do that, Tommy," Dad says. "If the thing breaks..." He takes a breath. "Let's keep everything else the same, at least for a minute."

I sit the chair upright.

"*Sarah* is leaving us," I tell Dad.

Elsa looks at me like, *Don't say it like that.*

"To give you two space," she says.

"Plenty of space, now," Dad says, then clears his throat. He snaps a look at me. "But you're staying?"

"Nowhere to go," I say. "Nowhere to be."

We eat in silence—my father across from me, Elsa holding her plate close to her face while she stands with her back to the bend of the kitchen counter, between the stovetop and sink.

❖❖❖

AFTER NOON, DAD STANDS in the doorway to my bedroom. He asks Elsa, "You have everything?"

"I do," she says, standing up, pulling the handle out of her red roller bag.

I'm already standing, staring at my poster of The Beatles, the one my mother gave me for my fourteenth birthday: Shea Stadium; Tuesday, August 23, 1966.

"From Mom," I say.

"I remember," he says. It's a minute before he says to Elsa, "Ready when you are." Then he turns and goes.

❖❖❖

ON THE WAY TO the airport, Dad says, "They'll cremate her tomorrow." The words create pressure in my head. First it's like fingers pressing my temples. Then my entire skull. I ball

up my left fist and put it in my right hand and squeeze as hard
as I can, making my teeth clench. "Then another day, and we
can pick her up."

◆◆◆

First we drop my rental car at the airport, then circle back
to drop Elsa off for her flight. It's Dad who pulls her luggage
from the trunk and sets it curbside.

"You're all set?" he asks.

Elsa says yes.

Dad tells her, "I have to say, I dread going back to that house."

Elsa reacts by launching herself at my father, wrapping
her arms around his neck. She presses her cheek against
his collarbone.

When she lets go, she turns and takes the handle of her
bag and heads toward the glass doors that separate when she
gets close. I catch up with her right inside the door and stand
in front of her so she can't easily pass.

"I'm sorry and goodbye," Elsa says.

Two days ago, I wanted her gone, wished I'd never met
her. But now she's the only Sarah who ever met my mother.
I don't know how to say goodbye, or how to act or react,
so what I do is hug her with everything I've got.

"Oh," she says. Then, "Thomas?"

I hug her like it'll bring my mother back to life. Like the
real Sarah isn't far, far away.

"*Thomas?*"

"Yeah?"

"You're kind of crushing me."

◆◆◆

BACK IN MY FATHER'S car on our way home, Dad says, "That's a darling girl. Whoever she is."

I don't respond. I'm too busy looking out the window at the flat, expansive, prosaic nothing. Bland scenery that's comprised of brown-green, highway-side grass, billboards with numbers I hope I never call, and colorless cars infinitely exiting and appearing.

❖❖❖

THAT NIGHT, MY FATHER orders Imo's Pizza and we eat it at the kitchen table without plates.

"I'd like to come to California soon," Dad says. "If that's okay with you."

"It is."

"You wouldn't be too embarrassed by your old man?"

I laugh a very small laugh, almost a hiccup, then suppress it. I'd much rather swim in this rare, quiet pain than let anything free me.

"And call whenever," I say. "Call all the time."

"I might," my father says.

Which reminds me: I've yet to charge my dead phone.

My father scoops up a middle square of pizza and looks at it. Then drops it back into the box. "Tomorrow your mother will be ashes," he says, and rubs one palm against the other to clear it of the breaded sand from the pizza crust.

❖❖❖

THE NEXT MORNING, LIKE yesterday, and every second since my mom passed, every single motion I make feels willful—a consciousness to every breath and blink. I'm careful when I go into my roller bag to find a clean T-shirt, clean boxers. As I airlift them clear of the surrounding clothes, I listen for every flit and crinkle.

"Your mother is ready," my father says from my doorway, and for just a flash I think she's alive. That they're going to the store. But then I know, it's her ashes, at the crematorium. A single word comes to my tongue, but I don't say it: *sift*.

"I can't go alone," Dad says.

I stand, grab my shoes. Go to the bed to put them on.

"Well, put on some pants, first."

❖❖❖

ON THE WAY BACK from the crematorium, Dad tells me, "She didn't want a funeral."

Mom, the only child of an only child. Dad's childless brother Chuck living on a farm in the middle of Oregon.

"I'll call Chuck and tell him," Dad says. "We don't need people flying all over the place. Nobody wants that."

❖❖❖

MOM'S ASHES SIT IN an urn on the coffee table. It's granite colored, a narrowed neck with a flat lid.

"I figure you'll head home soon," Dad says.

"What if I stay?" I ask. Because why go anywhere, anymore?

"Then you stay," he says.

He stands up, kisses his fingers, and holds them on top of Mom's urn until his eyes go red.

❖❖❖

IT'S DUSK WHEN I plug in my phone in the kitchen and watch as it powers up. When it's fully on, an alert sounds: sixteen new voicemails. All from Ryan.

Instead of listening, I call him back.

"Thomas, hey," he says. "Sorry to keep calling. You get my messages?"

"Messages," I repeat.

"Yeah," he says, hesitant. "It's just EO was pressing. Anarchy's very keen, but they're playing it patient. And I'm sure this isn't at the front of your mind, if you're thinking about it at all, so I'm sorry to be calling, really. I just…"

"Your messages," I interrupt, letting the last *s* create a tingle on my tongue.

"Right," he says. "EO wants to buy outright, Anarchy wants us to write the script."

"Okay," I say.

"So, yeah, we just need to make a decision. I left the numbers on your voicemail," he says.

"The numbers," I say.

"Yeah, EO's saying a hundred and twenty-five thousand."

"That one, then," I say.

"Right, but while Anarchy's half that, we'd get points on the back end. *If* it gets made."

"That one, then," I say.

"Well," he asks. "Which 'that one'?"

Outside I see a flicker of movement through the kitchen window. I look up, and in a wash of moonlight, against the backyard's back fence, standing with her back to me, amidst a bed of fading flowers, is Sarah.

"Thing is, you sell an idea, who knows where it ends up?" Ryan says. "So, I vote we write it."

I unplug my phone from the charger, push open the sliding glass door, the screen door after that. I step through the yard, eyes on Sarah.

"If we sell to EO, it's just a signature followed by an instant paycheck," he says. "But if we go with Anarchy, all we have to do is turn in a first draft to get paid. They'd give us twelve weeks. But it means you'd need to come home."

I'm about to tell him *EO*. So I don't ever have to go back to San Francisco, so I don't ever have to go anywhere. That I am here, and it took me so long to get here, and now Sarah is here, too, so there's no longer reason, ever, to leave.

Then Sarah turns, standing amidst pink and purple flower blossoms, and my phone beeps a sharp warning—low battery. "So what do you think?" Ryan asks as she writes on the inside of her left forearm. She holds out her arm to show me two words: *Find me.*

"Where?" I ask Sarah.

"What?" Ryan asks me.

Sarah looks up at me with an eye roll, like I never get it.

"Find you where?" I insist.

"Dude, you okay?" Ryan asks.

Sarah writes on her arm without erasing. Then shows me: *Home.*

"Ground control to Major Thomas?" Ryan says.

Sarah takes a step back, then turns, and makes her way behind a wide pine whose lower foliage has gone brown.

"Home," I say.

"Home?" Ryan asks, while I follow Sarah's path.

"We write it," I say.

"Awesome," he says. "I was hoping you were going to say that."

As I arrive behind the tree, a hover of clouds turns the entire yard dark. For a moment I can see Sarah's outline, a fading sparkle on a backdrop of fence. Then she's gone.

"When do you think you'll come home, then?" Ryan asks. "And of course, no hurry, with the funeral and whatever else, I just..."

"I'm on my way," I tell him, as I stand in my parents' backyard, all alone.

THIRTY-FOUR

THE NEXT MORNING, DAD'S at the kitchen sink, watching the faucet fill and fill and fill the coffee pot. Lost in the gurgle of overflow.

"Dad?" I ask.

"Hmm?" he says, but doesn't turn or shut off the water.

Already, I can see a difference in him. A sort of slouch, his shoulders softened by the onset of loneliness.

I stand next to him and turn the faucet off. "I think it's clean," I say.

"Oh, yeah," he says. "I know that."

I put my right hand on his shoulder and with my left I reach for the coffee pot. Gently, I tip it over and spill out the clear water.

"I need to go home, after all," I say. I don't tell him why. How to explain?

"Of course," he says. "Let me say goodbye to your mother, and we'll get you to the airport."

I back away from the sink and watch Dad move into the living room. After a few seconds, I follow to find his fingertips on the top of Mom's urn. He turns them a little to the left, then to the right.

"It's not her," he says. "I know that."

I don't know if I should argue it is, or isn't.

"Will you be okay?"

"Debatable," he says, and reaches his free hand into his pocket for car keys. "But we'll see."

❖❖❖

FOR MY FLIGHT TO SFO, I check in on an automated machine. *No*, my bag hasn't been out of my immediate control. *Yes*, I packed it myself. *Yes*, I want to change my seat. *No*, I don't want to upgrade to Economy Plus for sixty-three dollars. On my way to the bag drop, I take in every face. I'm overwhelmed as I search for Sarah through security, and all the way to my gate.

❖❖❖

ONCE ON THE PLANE, my mind drifts to my mother lifting the photo album to her face and kissing the picture of Joshua. I turn to the man in the middle seat and tell him, "I don't know what's wrong with me, but I can't cry."

"Huh," he says.

I look down, concerned.

"Well," he says, searching. "There's no shame in it." Then a long pause. "What I'm saying is it's okay."

❖❖❖

AT THIRTY-SEVEN THOUSAND FEET, I pop a single stick of gum into my mouth—a method I learned from my mother to stop my ears from clogging from the pressure.

I flip open United's in-flight magazine, and according to the world map on page thirty-eight, it's clear that the Brazil bone used to be connected to the Cameroon bone. That the

Morocco bone was, at one time, connected to the District of Columbia bone. Now hear the word of plate tectonics.

I pop another stick of gum and see that there's a Niger and a Nigeria. That Uruguay doesn't touch Paraguay. In Iceland, when it's noon, in the ocean to the immediate west it's 10:00 a.m.

I swallow, which ignites a crackle and whinny inside my head.

Denmark owns Greenland, France owns Tahiti and Reunion, Morocco owns Western Sahara.

I pop another stick.

There's a country called Tajikistan, one called Comoros, a Mayotte. Madagascar lives on. There is no Yakutsk.

I slip the magazine back into the net pouch and tuck my wad of gum into my cheek. I try to sleep. To mute the hiss of engine noise, I put on earphones that I don't plug in. The flight lulls and sways. My mind is nowhere, all at once.

❖❖❖

WE LAND SAFELY AND softly. At SFO's baggage claim I'm the last one at the carousel. I wait a long time before I go to the luggage courier.

"Can I help you?" he asks.

I shrug.

"Well, let's see." He places a laminated card in front of me with photos of luggage. When I just stare, he uses the eraser end of a pencil to point to the different possibilities. When I don't react, he asks, "Which one is it?"

I point to a black Samsonite with a Push-Button-Handle and the SmoothRoller® system. "Not that one," I say.

"Okay," he says. "Then which?"

A few minutes later, he tells me my bag is on a flight that landed, two hours ago, in Austin.

"How does something like that happen?" I ask.

❖❖❖

I HOP THE BART train into the city. The whole ride I stare off, way off, waiting for Sarah to materialize.

Once I'm off the train and up the escalator, I stand on fractured concrete in bleaching sun. It occurs to me that I'm close enough to run home. Which I've never done. Which I'd never do. Until now.

THIRTY-FIVE

C OVERED IN SWEAT FROM my sprint home, I huff into my apartment to find Ryan on the couch in pajama pants, playing video-game soccer. He drops the controller and stands immediately at the sight of me, while the game plays on before him.

"Dude," he says.

"I ran."

"From the airport?"

On the television, his team of soccer players stand still while the opposition moves swiftly toward his net.

"Incoming," I say, and lazily point at the screen. Right when he turns to look, his opponent kicks a rocket of a shot that ticks off the inner post, then spins toward the center of the back of the net. The announcer declares, "Goooooooal!"

Ryan picks up the remote and turns off the TV. Then looks at me, gauging what to say or do next. A look of concern drifts across his face.

"Where's your luggage?"

"Lost."

"Shit. Come sit."

I walk over and drop onto the couch. Everything feels slow like it's happening underwater. Ryan sits, a cushion's width between us, and faces me.

"We can talk," Ryan says. "Or we can just do nothing."

I ease low into the couch, nearly on my back, and stare at the play of late-afternoon light climbing across the ceiling.

"The night she died, my mother sat next to me, showing me old photos. She told me her life story, an entire history I didn't know existed. The way she was remembering—it was like her entire past was right in front of her. Like if she reached out, she expected to touch it." I fold my hands so my thumbs meet at the bottom of my sternum. "It was like all these mysteries of my past, all these little uncertainties and mild confusions that I'd mostly dismissed or forgotten about, were answered all at once."

"That's good then, yeah?"

I give a light shrug. I want to tell him that I have to find Sarah. But I don't want to argue. So I keep it to myself.

We sit quiet for what feels like a very long time. I breathe in and out and try to count the number of times I blink before Ryan breaks the silence. I lose track around fifteen.

"Do you want some water?" he asks.

I nod, and he gets up and heads to the kitchen. He returns with a liter-sized bottle of Poland Springs. He hands it to me after he twists off the cap. I take a long drink that goes down cold.

"Crisp," I say.

❖❖❖

STILL ON THE COUCH a few hours later, Ryan sets a bowl of pasta down on the coffee table for me. Cavatelli, my favorite.

"Little hollows," I say. There's spinach mixed in, and it's topped with chopped tomato.

Ryan sits and looks at me, serious, while I eat. He says, "I think maybe it's time for me to move out."

So this is how everything falls to zero. I drop the fork into the bowl with a clang and stop eating.

"I've just been here a long time, and right now I'm not sure if me being around will do any good."

I hold up the bowl of cavatelli he's made me—an argument against him leaving; a show that he's doing good.

"Okay, sorry," he says. "But only if you're sure."

As I lower the bowl, the fork squeals along the edge, then stills. I stab it into the noodles.

"I'm sure," I say, with my mouth full.

"I can't tell you how good it is to have you back here," he says.

I tell him, "I can't tell you how it feels to be home."

THIRTY-SIX

THE NEXT MORNING, A Sunday, Ryan's still asleep when I place my laptop on the kitchen table. I open it for the first time in five days, and as it powers on, I feel a shortness of breath, afraid I'm denying the potency of this larger moment. Reality is, I'm unready to reengage with the wider world via type and text. So when I see my email inbox has sixty-two new messages—a mix of invitations for contract work and complaints that I'm unresponsive—I ignore them all and shut my computer down.

I head to the cafe down the street where Ryan and I have gone every morning to hash out Elvis ideas over coffee. On my walk over, I wonder if Sarah will be there, waiting. But she's isn't. The late-morning sun's white heat reaches through the high windows and the same barista who's here five days a week, with his bushy beard and tattoo of an anchor on his forearm, says, "Hey, dude, where you guys been?"

I put up a quick wall between me and these last days, so I can't see, then tell him, "The moon." He laughs, but because there's no one behind me in line, and the people at tables are out of earshot, and because he's been kind to me in the past, I volunteer, "Actually, I went home to see my mother after way too long."

"I feel you."

For whatever reason, I expect him to ask if we were close. He doesn't, but I answer anyway. "Were we?" I say aloud. "We absolutely were."

In response to his puzzled expression, I ask for an iced tea and the last blueberry muffin. Then I sit where Ryan and I usually sit. Because today is any other day. Because everything is *just fine*.

❖❖❖

I'M STANDING OUTSIDE THE cafe with nowhere to be when a taxi stops in front of me, and out comes a family of four. The father gets the kids—a boy and a girl, both no older than eight—to the sidewalk, while the mother pays. She leaves the rear door open and tells me, "All yours."

Maybe this is how I find Sarah?

I get in, pull the door shut.

"Where to, my man?" the driver says. A black guy wearing a military-style olive hat.

"No idea."

"Top of the Mark it is," he says, certain.

"Fine," I say, and off we go.

We climb and dip through the rolling streets, and after a few blocks he asks, "You know how it got its name?"

"Who?"

"The Top of the Mark."

"I don't."

"Back in thirty-nine, a hotelier turned the penthouse of the Mark Hopkins Hotel into a cocktail lounge. Told a friend, 'I don't know what to call the top of the Mark.' And his friend said, 'Well, that's it.' The hotelier didn't get it. 'What's *it?*' he asked, and his friend said, 'Top of the Mark!' You believe that shit?"

I laugh an obligatory laugh, then look outside and glance at faces that aren't Sarah as we pass yellow and baby-blue and red-painted homes. When we turn roughly onto Market Street, I ask him, "What else you got?"

"That's why I'm takin' you there. That's all I know. Plus, you can have a drink to celebrate."

"Celebrate?"

"Always something to celebrate," he says. "And if you're flying low, then drink to being alive. No small miracle in that."

❖ ❖ ❖

OUT OF THE ELEVATOR at The Top of the Mark, I exit on to soft, reddish carpet with yellow flowers. It's a 360-degree view, and I go right up to one of the windows—facing west—and look out over the daylit city, the whites so crisp they sparkle. A waitress asks, "Can I get you anything?"

"A drink to celebrate," I say.

"Oh," she says, and switches course by tucking away the food menu, and holding open a menu that tells me they have over one hundred different types of martinis.

I ask her favorite.

"The opening page shows the ten most popular."

"But yours?" I say.

"I usually just close my eyes and point," she says, a strained smile.

When I look at the menu, flip a few pages, she excuses herself, tells me she'll be right back. Inside I find a Sunsplash and the Key Lime and the Vanillatini. All of them identically priced: fourteen dollars.

When the waitress returns and asks, "What can I get you?" I look down at the tops of my shoes, at the lush carpet.

"I guess I'm afraid that if I drink I could miss some surprise pain. Or wash away some notion or moment," I say.

"Okay," she says slow, with a frown, and goes back on her heels.

"Conversely, if I drink, I risk amplifying those same elements to the point where they'll deafen." I check my watch. "Since it's only eleven in the morning, let me wander. Maybe I'll come back."

Her eyebrows furrow and she forces a smile when I hand her the menu. I head toward the elevator. It's nearly all the way closed when I arrive, so I stick my hand in. The twin doors, decorated in what appear to be black beads, separate. I take a step back, preparing for Sarah. But inside, alone, is a woman who's maybe thirty, wearing a black sweater over a red dress covered in white circles.

I wave an apology as I enter, and she smiles with pursed lips and looks down. The dark wooden walls of the elevator are accented by lighter-brown ropelike decorations. There's a green number embedded in a black box above the door. It starts to count down from eighteen.

"This elevator's so nice," I say, as the number turns to four. "Have you been in it before?"

I look at her, and she looks back surprised. Like I wasn't seriously asking. "Excuse me?" she says, finally.

"My mom would have loved it."

We come to the ground-floor stop. I wait so she'll exit before me. Her strapless heels clap against the floor. "Bye," I say.

She turns with a closed-mouth smile, then tells me, "Bye."

THIRTY-SEVEN

BACK HOME FROM TOP of the Mark, Ryan's talking into a headset, staring at his smartphone's screen with great focus. "I'm looking at it," he tells whomever he's talking to. "I keep hitting refresh because I'm convinced it's fake."

I drop my keys on the couch-side table with a metallic clatter, and when Ryan hangs up, he holds up his phone for me to see.

"Look," he says. "It's unbelievable. Like, I really cannot believe it."

I look at his phone to see a page on Variety.com about the new, scripted shows that Netflix is considering for pilots in advance of the new fall season.

"Scroll down," he says. Amidst eight other descriptors I find:

Pilot

Written by Ryan Ahearn

"Post-modernist irony touches down"

This zany sitcom follows the lives of four diverse and disparate personalities angling to advance their collective careers by conjuring up the perfect reality television show. This quartet of thirty-somethings engage in audacious episode-to-episode exploits that eventually serve as fodder for their varied and often surreal television pilot ideas. If the network TV execs ever get on board with this ensemble cast's vision of the future of television, their careers will take flight!

When I'm done reading, I look up at Ryan wide-eyed and tell him, "That's you."

"It's *nuts*, right!?" he says. "We all get time to do rewrites with a director, then Netflix picks their three favorites to make into pilots. Oh, my god, I'm freaking out."

"Wow," I say, quiet.

"This is huge!" he says. "But there's a catch."

I wait.

"I have to go to LA," he says, cringing for my benefit. "But it should only be two weeks. Though maybe three? I'll basically just bury myself in rewrites."

I nod.

"Which means you'd have to write *Attack on Graceland*'s first pass on your own."

I nod, again.

"But that's a *tall* task, considering you've never written a script before."

I nod one more time.

"Or we could postpone," he says. "But as we're first-time feature writers, and Hollywood is fickle as fuck, that feels like a risk."

I stare at him, blinking.

"But I think you can do it," he says. "Don't you?"

I nod. My thinking is: if we get me jump-started by cracking into it first thing tomorrow, and if we work on it until he leaves, I should be okay.

"You sure?"

I nod again, now certain.

"I leave tomorrow, *early*," he says. "A meeting with the director first thing after I land, then writing sessions that'll go hard all week. And tonight I need to read it over and jot down notes upon notes."

Now, I'm triply unsure.

"But I'll be back," Ryan says, hands out to put me at peace. "Sooner than later." He grabs me by the shoulders, a ball of excitability. "I can't believe this is all happening at once!" He lets go and heads to the kitchen. I stay put. He shouts so I can hear him. "And while Anarchy money's not coming in for a few months, I've got rent covered! So you can ignore job offers, and hunker down to focus on Elvis!"

Which relaxes me.

Ryan comes back in with a bowl full of cinnamon cereal and asks me, energy still at a ten out of ten, "What about you? You get up to anything today?"

"I wandered," I say. I give a paced recap and mention my drop in to the Top of the Mark, and the woman in the elevator.

"You talk to her?"

"Kind of."

"Did you like her?"

I shrug. I didn't think anything about her beyond she was there.

"We should find her," he says, as he takes a bite of cereal. "Y'know, stake her out."

I give him a look.

"I'm *kidding!*"

Still, he sets his bowl of cereal next to his open laptop and starts typing.

"Don't," I say, like he's going to email her direct.

"Just come look."

I see Ryan's at craigslist.org. "Missed Connections," he says.

"Mixed what?"

"My sweet, flip-phone-using friend," Ryan says as he clicks and clicks. "This has been around for the last fifteen years, so of course you wouldn't have heard of it."

"Har, har."

"What color was her hair?" he asks.

"Why?" I ask and slump onto the corner of the table and sigh a sigh of tortured disinterest.

"Because you're miserable for good reason, and maybe this will help."

"Her hair was...spiderweb spun charcoal," I say to be difficult.

Ryan starts to type. "What else?"

"Did you write that?"

"What else?"

"She was, maybe, five eight? She was wearing... Wait, why?"

"Tell me what she was wearing!"

"A black sweater," I say. Then squint as I recall the dress. There were no navy flowers. No slapping ripple. "A red dress," I say in a fog. "With white circles."

"Thank you."

There were no ankle straps on her high heels. No buckle.

"All I really said to her was *bye*."

He types more, then I see him click [**publish**]. He turns and tells me, "Congratulations. **Elevator Girl at Top of the Mark** is your first ever Missed Connection."

THIRTY-EIGHT

IN THE WAY-EARLY MORNING, in my all-black room with my door closed, the light off, and my laptop screen dim, I click around on Missed Connections. As far as I can tell, it's a litany of anonymous, quick-hit posts from shy, unsure idealists who, when they had the chance, didn't meet or get contact info from a person that had them starry-eyed. So they hurried to Craigslist to post last-ditch headlines like:

I served you at my pizza restaurant (m4m)

I was your taxi driver (m4w)

You started talking to me about my poetry (w4m)

All followed by optimistic write-ups detailing their missed opportunity.

And now, amidst those who went public with their romanticized hope, Ryan's placed me.

I hear him up, prepping for his 6:00 a.m. flight, so I go to his room.

"Hey," he says, as he finishes packing for LA. "You're up stupid early."

It's a few minutes after 4:00 a.m.

"The girl from the elevator," I say. "What if she doesn't know Missed Connections exists?"

"Everyone knows it exists."

"I didn't."

"Everyone else, then," he says. "She hasn't replied?"

"No response," I say, relieved that she hasn't.

"Well, that's done, then," he says. "But I mean, if she had written, it'd be sort of fun, right?" Ryan says as he zips up his roller bag. Then wheels it past me into the hall.

"But there's no...*glue*," I say.

Which stalls him. His arms go wide. "No *glue?*" Ryan says and turns, put off. He looses a *pfft*, followed by a headshake, then heads to the kitchen.

I stay put, trying to define it. "No *life* to it."

I hear the faucet go on then off, then the sound of a glass being set on our metal dish rack. "So you're saying you need to meet a girl on a tightrope over a pit of starving crocodiles. Or equivalent. Got it."

"It should just be *more*," I say.

He comes and puts his hands on my shoulders. He looks me in the eyes and asks, "You okay? With your mom and everything?"

I seriously consider his question, which makes me space out. I race past the sight of Sarah's arm-written *Find me*, drift through an image of my mom's hand on my leg at home. I try to imagine a ledge I can grab hold of, or a space of flat, safe earth I can stand on. "I mean..." I start, expecting some words to follow, but there's none. Just a feeling of floating. Of drift. So I'm silent.

"I hate that I have to head out," Ryan says to me, after a squeeze of my shoulders. "But if you need me, just say so. I know it's a hard time, but I'm close. A short flight."

He grabs his laptop bag and puts it on his shoulder.

"I should be fine," I say.

"Sure," he says. "But nothing's ever so easy."

THIRTY-NINE

IN THE DAYS AFTER Ryan leaves, home is still, is stale, and I find myself trapped in a pinwheel loop of recent imagery: Mom laughing at dinner; Mom's thumb running over Joshua's photograph; Sarah standing in moonlight; Dad's hand atop Mom's urn; Mom laughing at dinner; Mom's thumb running over Joshua's...

For relief, I don't write the first draft of *Attack on Graceland*, as I promised myself and promised Ryan. Instead, a different, shameful pattern emerges: I shower, dress, head outside with brittle-feeling bones wrapped in thinning skin. I board a bus and embark on a directionless, all-hours sift through the city's seven-by-seven miles. All in a search for Sarah, in the hopes that I will find her and she will assuage my grief.

Like yesterday and the day before, and all last week, the bus predictably jerks, sputters, and rumbles, but this morning it smells like sweat and rust and rainwater rot. I breathe shallow through my mouth and distract myself from the scent by pressing my thumb into the oven's vanishing burn on my wrist, so it'll stay. So it'll scar.

When the bus wheezes to a stop downtown, I shoot off, eager for an uncontaminated breath. I wander aimless, until I find myself stalled on Second Street, between Mission and Market, by a glittering sidewalk that flashes and sparkles like a Paparazzi welcome. There I lean against a brick building and watch people cascade by. Frustrated because I haven't located unfindable Sarah, I start to create new possibilities by jotting down details of passersby. Just now, one jogs by at full speed with blue Adidas wristbands. Then a woman in a skirt and beat-up ballet flats flashes a glance at me as she strides by. I scribble down a single specific: the Long Island-shaped birthmark on her left calf.

After two hours, I take the bus back home. En route, I flip through my notes from the last three days—Valencia Street between Fourteenth and Eighteenth, the center of Ghirardelli Square, at Lotta's Fountain—to find a list of specifics that caught my eye. Curly red hair, railroad-spike cuff bracelet. Lime-painted fingernails, and cleft chin. Graceful strides, dark red lipstick.

Once home, once again, I don't open the blank Final Draft file labeled **Attack on Graceland 1st Draft.fdx** so I can type out the opening scene. Instead, I call my dad for my quick, semi-daily check-in, then slump onto my bed and stare at the ceiling, with my notebook open next to me. I watch as the sunlight reflects off the hardwood floor and swirls around the upper corners of the room. I try to remember how I felt *before*. Before Sarah. Before Mom got sick. Before Dad was alone from now on. Was I happy? Was I ever happy? Was I content or fulfilled? I remember myself as waiting. Waiting until. Waiting for. Then Sarah arrived, and every day after went by in a snap.

My phone rings, Ryan calling. I answer with a slow hello.

"Everything good?"

"The best," I say.

"Script coming along?"

"I'll say, yes."

Ryan laughs, and tells me, "Looks like I'll be gone another week. The director and I are digging deep, and it's hard. It's fun, *really* fun. It's just so busy! And the script's definitely okay?"

"Peachy and keen," I say, while I think: *Tomorrow I'll head in the direction of Coit Tower. The day after, the Ferry Building. The day after that, the de Young Museum.*

"Good, good," he says. "Oh, and Elsa and I were texting today. She hopes you're okay."

A surprise jot of light skitters across the ceiling. I watch its anxious, erratic dance. "I wish you were here to see this."

"See what?"

"Just the ceiling."

"Oh," he says with a laugh. "Me, too?"

FORTY

W HEN I PULL MYSELF out of bed, I don't type out the title page for *Attack on Graceland,* or start on scene headers, or write any dialogue back-and-forths. Instead, I open my notebook to scribbles everywhere, and because so far Sarah's nowhere, I take control by picking out a highlight from yesterday afternoon's page—*gray bell-bottomed pin-striped pants + "Are You Jesus?" T-shirt + tube-sock covered arm up to the elbow*—and use it to create the headline I type into Missed Connections:

Arm-Sock Girl at 826 Valencia (m4w)

I follow up by typing a rundown of her clothing, write that we were both at 826 Valencia's Pirate Supply Store in the late afternoon—while I looked through a drawer of eye patches, she covered her mouth while laughing at a drawer full of X's that mark the spot.

I click submit and type in my five-letter verification. I accept the terms of use, then in comes an email with a link inside. I click the link to confirm the listing, and my post goes live.

Then I flip back a few days in my notebook and pinpoint *red sweater with secondhand denim + beet-red messenger bag + hair trapped in white bandana* for the headline:

Bandana'd Damsel on Folsom (m4w)

I go through the motions—near Edwin Klockars Blacksmith Shop just after 9:00 p.m.; you asked me directions to the Jackson Brewery Complex—then I submit, verify, accept terms of use, click a link to confirm.

From a list of at least a dozen others, I pick one from today—*black pants/boots/hair, Middle Eastern (?), reading New Yorker.*

Then my phone rings. It's Ryan calling.

I seize up, and my eyes lock on to the ATTACK ON GRACELAND folder on my desktop that holds the unopened file, where all of our notes are collected. To curtail immediate script-related questions—*How's the writing going? What scene are you on?*—I answer with, "How's LA?"

"It's good!" he says, cheery. "I had a moment to breathe, and because I'm feeling guilty that I've left you on the hook for the script, I did a mini-brainstorm earlier and wanted to dump some Elvis ideas on you to keep you motoring. All which you can take or leave."

"Shoot," I say, holding my breath.

"I thought earlier that the crowd that gathers outside could be a character. Like, maybe they influence what the media's reporting, and that keeps changing? It seems funnier in my head. There are the usual fans and media, but what about the police first, like we talked about? And then maybe the FBI shows? Oh! And what if Lisa Marie Presley is behind it? Like, she *wants* the aliens there—maybe she used satellites to contact them? I don't know, that's stupid. But with Graceland's profits slumping, she knows aliens showing up will make international news. And since all press is good press, that'll reinvigorate people's appetite for Elvis. But, then maybe she has to confess to the FBI—because they're about to leave, maybe? I don't know. But everything she planned is fucked because the aliens are a literal threat to steal her pop's home? Does any of this make sense?"

"I get it," I say, but when I scan back through his ideas, all I can remember is: the crowd is a character, Lisa Marie Presley and the FBI. And Ryan asking if it made sense.

"Cool, cool," he says. "I'm just getting anxious because I'm buried in Netflix stuff that I can't get away from and I just really want us to nail this."

"Of course."

"All good with you, by the way? Just, with the script and everything else?"

"Keeping busy," I say. I ease my notebook closed, ashamed I'm letting him down. "Or at least I'm keeping distracted."

"I know it's been a rough ride," he says. "It's good to hear you're in motion."

FORTY-ONE

A FEW DAYS LATER, after three weeks away, Ryan calls to tell me he'll be back home in San Francisco tonight.

"Let's go grab a drink," he says, and when I don't immediately say yes, he asks me, "At least one?"

As soon as we're off the phone, it hits me that, *oh, fuck,* I've lost three weeks to Missed Connections, so I finally open Final Draft and create a title page. I stare at the screen, uncertain. It takes a few, wasted minutes for me to will away a sense of overpowering exhaustion before I force myself to type:

INT. GRACELAND GIFT SHOP—DAY

LUCAS RAMSDELL (33), a handsome, slim man with a full head of brown hair and an outdated seventies style, shadily walks around the gift shop before he slips a pair of silver imitation Elvis sunglasses into his jacket pocket.

An overweight Graceland employee—white, female, all business—hurries toward Lucas.

                    EMPLOYEE
          Sir. Sir.

Lucas holds his arms wide, a show of innocence.

> LUCAS
> You got the wrong guy!

The woman pushes past Lucas.

> EMPLOYEE
> Sir, those are Christmas ornaments not
> earrings!

The woman is talking to a man who is hooking a Graceland ornament into his eight-year-old daughter's earlobe.

I will myself to keep going, but I'm drawn toward the pulsing lure of my Missed Connections notebook, a distraction that's replaced my fruitless search for Sarah. I crack it open and like that—it's two hours later—and all I've got to show for my misspent time is a sense of shame and seventeen new Missed Connections posts.

I get a text from Ryan saying he's just off his plane at SFO and he'll be home in half an hour. I close my laptop and sit back, as a scream of guilt sounds off in my chest. I take long deep breaths, and it's only a few seconds before the Mom-inspired cycle of the pinwheel starts anew: Mom turning the corner when I first arrived; Mom shouting out, "Hot-wired the son of a bitch!"; Mom kissing Carl's picture; Dad telling Elsa, "I dread going back to that house."

❖❖❖

THAT NIGHT, RYAN AND I end up at a cocktail bar a few blocks from our place. While he's at the bar ordering our first round of drinks, I jot down the particulars of a girl across the room—*oval face, glow-in-the-dark pale, Ukrainian flag necklace*—when Ryan returns and tells me, "All work and no play makes Thomas a poor drinking companion. Away with the notebook!" I tuck it inside of my jacket, then Ryan gets quiet. "How are you, really?"

I nod.

"We haven't really talked about it. Which is my fault. It's hard to know when to press, or let you breathe. But I'm here to talk. In case you want to."

I shake my head. "I don't," I say. "Not yet." Though the truth is more like, *Not ever.*

Ryan nods. "Well, the offer stands. Anyway, how's the script coming?"

"I should be further along," I say.

He laughs. "Everyone who's ever written anything thinks they should be further along. How far did you get?"

Instead of dropping the bomb that I'm a half page in, I lie and tell him I'm up to page nine.

"*Oh,*" he says, clearly concerned, then tries to mask it by shaking the ice in his drink and staring into it. Then he turns and looks at me. "Well, it's a start. And I'm sure those nine pages are tight. Send me what you have and I'll read it."

"Not yet," I say.

"I totally get that," Ryan says. "But time's *flying.* I just want to make sure... I mean, you get the story, probably better than I do. But don't worry about being meticulous. Show me stuff, even if it's just the bones." He pauses, and his lips go to the side. When he's anxious, he chews the inside of his mouth. "I'll crack on with Netflix, so we can do the rest together. But I'm here, y'know? I'm on your side. The more you share, the easier it is for me to keep the ball rolling once *Pilot's* finished."

"I get it," I say.

"Okay, cool," he says, relieved by my getting it. "Anyway, I'm glad you came with me tonight. I wish we'd done this more when I was first back, but heartbreak and thinned-out bank accounts... But it's good to be out and meeting people."

But I'm out all the time, intentionally *not* meeting plenty of people.

"These two," Ryan says, and gestures in the direction of a pair of women wearing colorful, flowing dresses cut just below the knee. Before I can say no, he waves when they look in our direction.

"Dude," I say.

"Excuse me," he says to one of them.

"Let's not," I say.

"Excuse me!" he repeats to the women as he stands. "I'm sorry, but there's space if you'd like to join us." They pause, look at one another. "If you sit with us, you'll get to meet my best friend. And he's wonderful."

The blonde shrugs and says, "Sure." The dark-haired one follows.

After preliminary hellos with Colette (blonde) and Gemma (dark-haired), Ryan orders a round of cocktails for the table, then sells me by saying I'm the mastermind behind a movie concept we sold, and, no thanks to him, I'm now writing the first draft solo while he flits around LA.

"It's your idea?" Gemma asks me. Her dark hair is pixie-cut, her teeth perfectly straight.

"Ryan and I thought it up together."

"So humble," Ryan says as he puts his hand on my shoulder. "So talented at deflecting credit."

The girls laugh.

❖❖❖

I'M MIDWAY THROUGH MY second Vodka Collins, feeling lighter and freer than I have since LA, the night with Carly before

Sarah showed. But amidst this light and free, what makes the most sense is to excuse myself from talking to Gemma so I can rush home, go to Craigslist so I can:

[post], Gemma...(m4w), [publish].

But in lieu of a rattling exit, I interrupt all conversation to announce that I have a theory in progress.

"*Oh?*" says Gemma.

"*Oh?*" says Ryan, mimicking her.

"Do these theory announcements happen often?" Colette asks Ryan.

"She means '*Oh?*'" Gemma says. "Now spill it."

With the blustering fuel of alcohol swimming in my veins, I say like it's a conspiracy, "It's my Collision Theory." Everyone leans in. After weeks of intentionally talking to no one, their curiosity and interest surprise me. "Say I'm at a dinner party."

"Potluck or...?" Gemma interrupts. "*Kidding.* Sorry. Go on."

"Okay, so I'm at a dinner party, and there's a girl next to me, and we end up talking. She and I are simply a *meet.*"

"Totally," Colette says. "She sounds boring anyway."

They all laugh. I trundle on. "Everything is based on the impact of molecules," I say. "Because I was invited to this dinner party by friends, the impact of molecules is lessened. So my theory is that for a meaningful, deep-rooted relationship to form, the initial intersecting of two beings has to be a collision, with surprise and randomness, where things are thrown way off the tracks."

"That's the most elegant rejection I've ever gotten," Gemma says.

More laughs.

"So are we all just a boring meet?" Ryan asks.

"It appears so!" Gemma says with a smile, and raises her glass, so they all do. I raise my glass last. "To be safe, let's gently toast with these glasses so none of them fall in love."

"If only I'd have slipped on an ice cube, barrel-rolled you both, and Thomas could have caught you to save the day," Ryan says.

"He might be right, though," Colette says. "My parents were a meet. Then I guess they *unmet* when they divorced." She laughs, and tells Ryan as an aside, "They haven't talked for years." Then she takes a long drink from her straw, emptying her highball glass so it's just a lime wedge and some defeated ice.

"I had a boyfriend once who was a *definite* collision," Gemma says. "Fireworks, then the ultimate flame-out. God, he was bad news in every direction. Such a total asshole." Her eyes go watery and dark. "So while I want to be a cool kid and say, *Yay, collisions!,* wisdom tells me a plain old-fashioned meet might suit me just fine."

"Lately I've been trying to replace a past collision," I say. "My thinking being that the only way to replace a collision is with another collision."

Gemma says, "Maybe you should consider changing your approach?"

"I know," I say. "But sometimes you start a thing, even if it doesn't feel good, even if it doesn't feel right, and it's like you have to finish to prove that it was all for something. Or maybe I just want to prove myself right."

"You know who else thinks that way?" she says. "*Gamblers.*"

FORTY-TWO

THE NEXT MORNING—MY HEAD singing and my stomach gurgling from downing four over-sugared drinks—I check my email to find my first-ever response to one of my many Missed Connection postings. It's from "Angela"—**Dark, Curly Hair, Holding a See-Through Bag of Kiwis on Fillmore**—and the subject line reads: *craigslist posting: i saw you too...* In the body of her email, she's written, "…and I liked your hair."

Surprised, I want to call out to Ryan to ask what I should do next. But I stop myself because the Elvis script is still on page one; because he'd know how I've been spending my days. Any possible positive dims, and instead of feeling found, I feel exposed and embarrassed. When I write back to Angela, all I can bring myself to type is: "Hi, I'm Thomas."

Which is enough.

❖❖❖

THE NEXT NIGHT, WHILE Ryan's up the street at our local café doing another pass on his Netflix pilot, I'm two miles from home, standing on the street with Angela, after dinner. She's wearing jeans and gray suede boots. There is no wind. "We can have a margarita there," she says and points to a Mexican-themed bar a few doors down, then to a wine bar across the street. "Or a glass of wine there."

"Either for me," I say with rare enthusiasm.

After all this looking for Sarah—*Find her*? Where?!—when Angela says, "Wine!" and loops her arm into mine, it ignites in me a starry explosion of romantic possibilities.

The late-October air is charged with a wintry chill, and as she leads me across the street I tell her it's funny how we met. How the cosmos couldn't account for the internet when the continents were being pulled apart. But here we are.

"Missed Connections are great," she says. "I'm on there all the time. It's how I met my boyfriend."

I stop, surprised.

Angela pulls at my arm with playful zeal. "Hurry up!"

But I don't budge.

"*Come on*," she says with a flirty pout.

"A boyfriend?"

Angela holds up her hand, shows me her wedding ring. "I feel like maybe you haven't noticed this," she says.

"You're married?" I ask.

"Not to my boyfriend."

She draws me closer to the curb. A car passes.

"To sum it up: I'm married to my husband Benjamin, I have a boyfriend Victor, and I'm on a Missed Connections date with you. The first two are one hundred percent in the know, and they're fine with it. Now you know, too."

I shake my head and look down. I'm surprised by how disappointed I am. Angela being little more than a stranger.

"Look, we're having fun, right?" she says. "So maybe we see what happens?"

But I know, now. This is no collision. I am no one to her, and she will be no one to me. The initial impact of our molecules was low-grade, but now it has flatlined to zero.

"Sorry," I tell Angela as I back away. "But I better not." Once there are a few meters between us, I turn and walk in the direction of my apartment, hands in pockets, head down against the cold, while the pinwheel spins.

❖❖❖

THE NEXT MORNING, I check my email to find **Subject: CL: Oh, hey!** from Cat. After the Angela twist ending, I'm reluctant to write back, but my thinking is, what if? Otherwise I have to write *Attack on Graceland*. And today? There's just no way. So, that night I'm nearly to the corner of Minna and Second Street, when a woman I've never seen before is waving in my direction. I look behind me, but she shouts, "Thomas!"

I'm confused, because in my mind Cat is **Short Black Hair, Surprise Blue Eyes from the Fulton 5 Bus**. But this girl's hair is light brown, not black. Her eyes, I see when we shake hands, are brown, not blue. My mind races, trying to match her to some past moment—some clerical notebook error on my part—but I feel certain this is the first time I've ever seen this woman in my life.

"So?" she asks as her left hand goes to her hip, and her right hand extends away from her in a show of beauty pageant mimicry.

Her *So?* is for how I think she looks, but shouldn't I already know? Still, I tell her, "Great." Because something in me won't break the illusion—maybe this wrinkle will serve as the surprise, the randomness that could add up to a collision.

"Tonight my work's office party is there," she says, and points to the Museum of Modern Art.

I give a surprised look.

"Skip the frying pan, straight into the fire," she says. "Might as well maximize potential awkwardness, right? Just don't be surprised if I introduce you as my fiancé."

"Really?"

"*Really?*'" she mimics, then laughs. "You're hilarious."

Once we're inside MoMA, we check in and grab glasses of Sauvignon Blanc. We walk around at a leisurely pace past handfuls of people, but Cat doesn't say hello to anyone.

"Are we crashing this party?" I ask.

"I wish," she says. "But no. I work at Morgan Stanley, so at things like this it's just wave after wave of somebodies."

We're standing before a piece of Gerhard Richter's work when Cat—who is Catarina, not Catherine—says to me, "You know, you're a lot more guarded than you were over email."

"Oh?" I say. My phone rings in my pocket, a vibration-pause-vibration, but I ignore it.

"With me, you can just say what's on your mind. I'm impossible to offend."

"Oh," I say. "Okay."

"So, go on..." she says.

"Well," I start. "You're not the girl that I saw on the bus."

"Does it matter?"

"I don't think so," I say.

"You must be *so* disappointed," she says and flicks her hair with a laugh. "I'm an absolute horror."

"You're not—you're obviously not."

"Look," Cat says. "I was on that bus at some point that day. So I clicked. It wasn't me, but my ego wanted to be picked at random from *all* the other girls in the city. And I'm sure that says something weird about me that I can dig into with my therapist. But it's all weird. Online dating. Craigslist. Meeting in person. Meeting at all. I just figured, I'm single and you're searching, so in a bold moment, I decided: Take a chance. Write and say hello, and just see."

"I get it," I say. "I appreciate you telling me."

But reality has set in: we are just two people who were on separate buses, brought together not by wondrous chance, but each of our flawed intentions.

"I guess I'm just not the Sarah you're looking for."

"What'd you just say?" I ask.

"I'm not the someone you're looking for?"

My hand goes to my forehead, a relief. I visibly exhale.

"You can go," she says, unaffected. "It's really fine."

But it doesn't feel fine. Sarah is nowhere to be found, my two Missed Connections attempts were total fails, and I feel singular in the world. Alone.

"In fact, I release you," Cat says as she leans forward and kisses me on the cheek. "Good luck, hopeful Thomas. Now if you'll excuse me, I'm going to drink too much wine and flirt with my boss's son."

Cat raises her glass with a wide smile, then walks away.

❖❖❖

ON MY DEFEATED WALK home, while the moon glows wide and yellow in the sky, a new pinwheel kick-starts: Mom kissing my forehead goodnight when I was seven; Dad lighting candles in January when I was ten… But before it's run a full cycle, it's stalled by a bus that slows to a crawl at a stoplight. I look inside and when I see her, she's looking right at me. I can't believe it. It's Sarah.

I raise my hand in slow motion, a still wave, then I realize, *no*, it's not Sarah. But this girl looks so much like her. It's maybe five seconds I study her, while she studies me. Then the bus chugs and stammers. As it pulls away, she waves back.

❖❖❖

AT HOME, BEFORE BED, I pull out my laptop and head to Missed
Connections, click on [**post**] and I write:

> **Window Wave from the Geary Bus (m4w)**
>
> **You were on the bus at the corner of Geary
> and 5th. I waved and, after a few confused (?)
> seconds, you waved back. You: Dark hair, slim
> neck. Your eyes were faraway diamonds. Me:
> I can't get my bearings. I'm in this giant, ongoing
> spin. What I want isn't just inaccessible, but she's
> long gone. Are you the one who can stop it? The
> solution to quiet everything down?**

FORTY-THREE

A WEEK LATER, RYAN'S cooking in the kitchen, taking a break from what he's calling *Pilot*'s final stretch. I hear my phone ring in my bedroom and race to answer, but don't get to it before it goes to voicemail.

I return to the kitchen to tell Ryan, "It was a call from Anarchy." I play him Sam's recorded voice, "Oy, mate, Sam here. Just a quick bell to see how the script's moving. Would love to see a few pages, geezer. The first act, if you've nailed it. Cheers."

I hang up, trying to hide my alarm, and look to Ryan for guidance.

"Producers," he says with a note of disapproval. "It's only been five weeks. I've never written anything resembling a readable script in less than eight. He's just amped, which is a good thing. But best for you to send it to me, and I'll read it tomorrow," he says. "Maybe we send a scene or two, but really, Sam can wait. We've got another seven weeks before it's due."

Which means I've burnt 41 percent of the time we've got to finish our first draft. And I've only done, roughly, 8 percent.

"Okay," I say, feeling hollow.

"And I'll be free by week's end. We'll be up against it time-wise, but we've got the blessing of working from what you've already done. Which'll make life way easier."

I don't tell him I'm still twenty-two pages shy of a finished first act. Ninety-two pages shy of a first draft. Or that the eight pages I've written may be totally worthless.

"Speaking of, I was thinking about how we could develop our reluctant sidekick character into the ultimate Elvis nerd," Ryan says. "Like, he'll know what movies to use for guidance to get him and Lucas out of jams in any given situation, but instead of a convenient hanger-on, he's an asset. We keep him dorky and weak, like we talked about from the start, so he can't save the day himself. But the audience sees him as an unsung hero. You've probably got something better than that, but, yeah."

"No," I say. Because I don't. "That's smart."

"It'll keep our main dude from having to learn all the Elvis stuff on the fly, which means we'll have to do less heavy lifting."

Ryan's just said more about the script in two minutes than I've typed in weeks. "Yeah," I say. "Sounds good."

"You want one of these?" he asks, and holds up a meatless hamburger patty that looks like a brown, soy waffle. I tell him no thanks and head out of the kitchen, for fear the *Attack on Graceland* chatter will turn to unanswerable specifics. But before I'm out of earshot, Ryan calls out, "Oh, and I wanted to ask you… Elsa's got a work thing in Seattle on Wednesday, then she's going to be in town for a long weekend, and… would it be weird if she stayed here?"

Elsa? The uninvited? Who played Sarah in a past life? Who knows my mom's tear ducts had clogged, that she left notes around the house for my helpless father? *"The* Elsa?"

"We were going to get an Airbnb, and we can, it's totally cool, but I wanted to ask you, since money's tight for the next while…"

"Elsa, though. Really?"

"*Really,*" he says, and I see in his eyes that this is a real thing. She's not just coming to San Francisco for a long weekend. She's coming to see *him.* He's invited *her.*

"She's..." I want to call her a wrecking ball. Or unhinged. But without her, maybe I would have never seen my mother. And she stayed and supported. Tried, and fought, when I wouldn't. "She's welcome."

"Yeah?"

I nod.

"She's really brilliant," he says. "I saw her a few times in LA. And unlike Delphine? Elsa actually likes me." There's delight in his eyes until he sees my face, the wrack of sadness over my mom, over Sarah. "Shit, sorry. I didn't mean to..."

"No," I tell him. "You're excited. It's good." Because it is good.

"You're *sure* she can stay?"

"Yeah," I say. "Of course." And it's true.

"Thank you," he says. "She'll be thrilled to see you."

Ryan turns and uses a spatula to smush down his burger patty, which hasn't snapped or sizzled. It's now darker, more solid. He moves it from grill to plate, and I see the non-meat doesn't leak any non-grease. He covers it with lettuce and a slice of tomato. I watch all of this from the doorway, see a lightness and a joy in him that I haven't seen for ages.

FORTY-FOUR

I T'S THREE DAYS LATER when my cell phone wakes me from an early-evening nap. It's Ryan calling.

"Hey," I say, face pressed into my pillow.

"You're sleeping?" he says.

"A little. What's up?"

"I'm at the airport and Elsa's plane is running late, so I'm killing time. And I don't mean to be up your ass, which, by the way, is a disgusting expression, but I just checked my email and you *still* haven't sent me the script."

"I know."

Just this morning, I inched it to page fourteen, only halfway through the first act, which is what he's expecting. "Just send whatever you have, so I can at least see."

"Soon," I say, buying whatever time.

"*Now!* Just send something. The first page. The first five. I've tried not to press because it's been a crazy time for you emotionally. But it's been six weeks, and for all I know you haven't typed a word."

"I have."

"Then prove it," he says. "This is a big deal for us. Or for me, if you want to bail. Elsa's here three nights, and once she's gone, we have to hit the ground sprinting if we're going to meet our deadline."

"I know," I say, feeling the mass of these wasted days.

"And if I'm going to be starting from zero, you have to tell me."

"It's not at zero," I say. But could be.

"Well you need to tell me if it is," he says. I consider my input so far, which has been passionless, distracted, and basic. But I'm too ashamed to confess. "Because I need to mentally prepare myself to take on the width of the entire Graceland load if that's what's needed."

"I'm telling you," I say. But I don't tell him anything.

"Okay," he says, assuaged. "Okay. I'm not trying to be a dick, it's just... Oh, wait..."

I wait. While I do, I hear a noise in the bathroom, or outside of the door. There's a noise somewhere.

"One sec!" he says. The chirp of chiming glee, brought on by Elsa's arrival, surges through my phone. I sit up and press the phone against my chest to mute it.

"Sarah?" I whisper in the direction of the French doors that separate my bedroom, separate myself, from the hallway's dusky haze.

I stand and stare out the window, listening.

Ryan says a muffled something. "What?" I ask, lifting the phone back to my ear as I head out into the hallway's dimmed light.

"Someone wants to say hello," Ryan says.

"Thomas," Elsa asks.

"Hey," I say into the phone, quietly, for fear that if Sarah is here, any noise could scare her away.

"Thanks for letting me stay. I know it's not... Y'know, after..."

"It's fine," I say, listening as I speak. "It's good."

"Good," she says, and chokes up a bit. "I'm so relieved to hear that. I'm looking forward to seeing you. *What? Okay, yeah.* Ryan told me to tell you we'll be back late. Or later. So, don't wait... Oh, no, stop! *Stop!*" There's a high squeal of laughter and release. "He's tickling me!" The connection dies.

"*Sarah?*" I say again, as I close my phone.

I listen, listen, listen.

But there is no sound.

There is no Sarah.

FORTY-FIVE

IN THE MIDDLE OF the night, my phone rings. I answer and a voice says, "Thomas?"

It's my mother.

I try to ask where she is, but my mouth won't open.

"Thomas, are you there?"

I try to make a sound with my throat, just to let her know it's me. But nothing comes out.

"That's too bad," she says.

In my head I'm shouting, *Mom! I'm here! Don't hang up! Mom, please! Please! Don't go! Don't go!*

"A real shame," my mother says. Then she hangs up.

I wake into morning light, breathing out the words *Don't go,* while tears stream down my face. Sad reality slowly sets in as I realize it's a dream, and that my mother is still gone. My pillow is sopped with tears. A release, finally. Though I can't stop shaking.

❖ ❖ ❖

I CALL MY FATHER to check in.

Dad sighs, then there's a long pause. He makes a clicking sound with his tongue, and I expect his usual: go quiet or change the subject. But then he speaks, an outpour. "I'm handling your mother's death very poorly, and it's getting harder," he says. "The woman deserves some peace. Christ, add it up: Carl; the miscarriage; Joshua; her cancer. But even so, I want her to come back to me and stay."

I want to tell him he can't think things like that. But why can't he, when for so long I have, with Sarah?

"Just last night, I cried my eyes out over the efficiency of the dung beetle," Dad says. "In the last six weeks all I've read are the backs of cereal boxes, wondering what the hell riboflavin does."

"Dad, I'm sorry."

"As for spilling guts, while I've got you on the phone, let's make it a double," he says. His tone shifts from self-pity to acute interest. "I've been meaning to ask you about Sarah."

Surprised I tell him, "Oh. Okay." Followed by a nervous exhale-laugh meant to indicate any talk of Sarah will lead down a series of disinteresting paths.

"Though I'll save us going in circles and ask what I really want, which is, What's going on with you?"

"Nothing," I say.

"Which we both know is bullshit."

He waits, but he's right, so I'm silent.

"The not coming home, I get," he says. "With what your mother was asking? But that girl—who was very nice, don't get me wrong. But I can't quite solve it."

"I didn't know she'd be there."

"*She*," he says.

"Sarah."

"*Right.* 'Sarah,'" he says, then takes in a deep breath and lets out a longer exhale. "If you're in trouble, Thomas… If you're struggling… I'm your father."

"I know," I say, wanting to ball up, to disappear.

"I know loss. I know vacancy to the end of this world and back. I'm telling you, you can talk to me."

"I will," I say. "I'll try."

I hear Dad's shallow breathing. The sound of him listening.

"Dad, if it'd help, you can come visit."

"I like the sound of that," he says. "I appreciate the invite. But be careful—where my head's at these days, I might just show up on a whim."

❖❖❖

WIDE AWAKE, I GET up, shower, then exit into crisp morning light to grab treats to make Elsa feel welcome, and to thank her—as lonely as I now feel—for leading me home.

I head downtown and grab three milk chocolate chip cookies from Specialty's, then hop the BART and head toward Craftsman and Wolves, a fancy-pants pâtisserie in the Mission. I'm lower than ever on funds and after Ryan's tongue-lashing, I'm hit with the full fright that if we don't submit a finished script to Anarchy in six weeks, there's no financial relief, no rent-funding windfall. Still, I go all out, and ask the barista to pick his four favorites. I end up with a Thai scone, a hazelnut financier, a cocoa-carrot muffin, and a muscovado morning bun.

❖❖❖

ONCE I'M BACK HOME, I thump up the stairs to my apartment, then noisily enter, an alert to everyone inside that I'm home. Once I'm in, Ryan approaches, all smiles. "And I thought we were up early," he says.

I hold up the three heaving bags of treats and tell him, "I brought you these. An Elsa welcome."

In the kitchen, I lay out the cookies and the pâtisserie sweets.

"Craftsman and Wolves!" Ryan says, impressed. "These look amazing."

I halve one of the chocolate chip cookies and offer it to him. "Not yet," he says. "I'll wait for her."

"Wait's over," Elsa says, sheepish, as she comes in wearing pajama pants with the different faces of US presidents. Her blonde-streaked hair is a bedhead fluster. She looks at me with an expression bearing every apology.

At first, I look down. Seeing her brings me back: her handing me my phone with my mom on the other line; her answering my parents' door before I knew she was playing the role of Sarah; the staircase with my parents, when I wouldn't let her pass.

"I got up to pee and heard you two talking," she says, so shy. "But I can come back in a bit."

"Not at all," Ryan says. But it's my permission she's after.

"Come in," I say. "Breakfast is served."

"He got us all this," Ryan says.

Elsa's face scrunches, a show of gratitude. "That's so sweet." Then she starts to cry. "Sorry."

"You okay?" Ryan asks, genuine in his concern.

She nods, then breaks off a piece of scone and takes a tiny bite.

I step to her and put my hand on her shoulder. "It's good to see you," I say.

She turns fast and hugs me, her arms over my arms, so I'm barely able to pat her on the back. Ryan looks at me like, *She's a prize.*

"It's good to see you, too," she says, then backs away and wipes her eyes. "And clearly some of us are emotional!"

We all laugh as Elsa takes another bite of scone and puts her hand on Ryan's back while she chews. "How's your dad?" she asks.

"I talked to him this morning," I say. "It's slow going."

"He's such a nice man," she tells Ryan. Then to me she says, "He's called me a few times. I hope that's okay."

"Of course," I say.

❖❖❖

I HEAD BACK TO bed for a bit and stare out of my open blinds. The clouds are a mess of cotton balls gummed together, the sun a fuzzy, gazillion-watt bulb. I think about my mother, the dream of her calling. My father, barely afloat. How my life right now feels like a slow train wreck with more carriages yet to crash.

Then my phone rings, a number I don't know. Area code **646**.

"I know it's early," a soft, vulnerable female voice says. "But last night I wanted to call, and didn't. And I told myself if I still wanted to call when I woke up then I would. Oh, this is Carly, by the way."

"Hey," I say.

"I'm in San Francisco for a conference. You free to meet up for a drink?"

FORTY-SIX

THAT NIGHT AT LATIN American Club, I find Carly at the bar, sipping dark booze from a short glass. I lift onto a stool so we're side by side, and without looking at me she says, "It's good to see you."

Before I can respond, a female bartender steps over and tosses a square, paper napkin into midair, so it spins, then lands soft in front of me. I point to Carly's drink and say, "What she's having."

"Jameson on the rocks," the bartender says, and spins away.

Carly turns to me and says, "I'm sorry about your mom."

"Thanks," I say.

"Oh, no," she says. "Does that mean she's gone?"

I nod.

"*Fuck*. I'm so sorry."

My drink arrives and I tell her the simplest version in the shortest time: "My father and I assisted her suicide. I should have gone home sooner." There's silence between us, until I tell her my mother once hot-wired a car in Frankfurt, Germany so she could drive to visit friends in Heidelberg.

"No way," Carly says.

"All facts," I say.

"Must've been an amazing lady."

My eyes well, but this time there are no tears. Carly raises her glass. We toast, and I drink.

"This is my favorite bar in town," Carly says. "Everywhere else the music's so loud, you have to scream."

I take note. The room's volume comes from the rumbling rise and fall of other conversations, shot through with the occasional cackle, or the crash of the bartender scooping ice.

We have a second drink. A third.

"It's so stupid we met this way," Carly says.

"What way?"

"*In person,*" she says, a mock scoff as she gets up to go to the bathroom. "We should have used the internet like everyone else. Since, y'know, it's simultaneously trained us to have disastrously astronomical expectations for love and the lowest expectations of all time. Which I think is just...super healthy." Carly laughs at her own joke then excuses herself.

Once Carly's out of sight, the bartender points to my glass and asks, "Another?"

"Three's my limit," I tell her, and it's true. My face is warm, and I feel pressure in the top of my head, like my scalp's trying to shift forward.

I sip from my drink then take a peek down the length of the bar to find Carly on her way back, only she's stopped, watching me from a distance. A look of stunned recognition's overtaken her face.

I give her a look like, *What?*

She holds my gaze as she steps forward, and once she's in earshot her shoulders slump and she says, "Oh, fuck."

"What?"

She lets out an exhale and puts the back of her hand to her forehead. "Oh, my god. We *have* met before."

I look at her face and wait for it to register. But it doesn't.

"*Fuck,*" she says, and barely shakes her head. Then she's so still.

"You okay?" I ask her.

"Are you?" she asks, then leans back and takes a deep, stuttered breath.

I don't know, now, so I don't answer.

"Of course you wouldn't remember," she says. And I race through, trying to find her in my memory, but it's all empty, it's all air.

Finally, she whispers, "The funeral."

My first thought is, *What funeral?* But then it hits me, so all I say is, "Oh."

"I need some air," Carly says. "Just a minute."

She hurries past me, out the front door. I watch her walk to the right, through the frame of the bar's wide window, an open hand on her forehead, until she's out of sight.

FORTY-SEVEN

A T THE FUNERAL, MEMBERS of her family took turns telling me why she took her own life. So convinced they understood the wirework of her mind.

At the wake, they found out I was the one who saw her jump.

❖❖❖

FAMILY AND FRIENDS ASKED, "Did she look unhappy?" "Was she beautiful?" "Had she cut her hair? It was getting so long."

I told them, "She looked like all you could ever want."

❖❖❖

"YOU COULD HAVE STOPPED her," a man said, his face pomegranate red. "You should have done whatever it took."

"I *tried*," I said.

I'd offered everything I had. Everything I was. With everyone in the room staring at me, with everyone judging, I realized it wasn't all that very much.

❖❖❖

A MIDDLE-AGED WOMAN PULLED me aside and looked at me with vague disappointment. She searched my face for answers, but there were no answers. "It's the most selfish thing a person could do," she said. "At least she could have left a note."

❖❖❖

A FAMILY FRIEND WANTED to know, "Did she say anything?"

I thought of a few lies to salve their wounds:

I am going to miss you all so much.

Tell everyone I love them.

I'm going to be very sorry.

I disappointed them by shaking my head. Because she didn't say any of it.

❖❖❖

"YOU'RE SO LUCKY TO have seen her."

"God help her."

"You could have done more."

"You're part of the family now."

"Was she crying?"

"How could you let this happen?"

"I think she was, well, you know, pregnant."

"I think she was, well, a coward."

"I think she was unwell."

"She was selfish."

"She was an angel."

"She was a time bomb."

"She was just like her mother."

"She was ours."

When they'd stopped talking, when the room had finally taken on a silence, and the younger handful of us that leaned against the room's walls looked down, embarrassed by the procession of know-it-alls, I took a breath.

I leaned to the woman next to me, late-twenties, hair a dishwater-blonde bob, an elaborate tattoo on the inside of her right forearm. I asked, "How did you know Sarah?"

She leaned in, confused, and asked me, "Who's Sarah?"

FORTY-EIGHT

When Carly returns to the bar, she slides onto the stool next to me and takes a long, slow drink. She sets her glass back down on a damp napkin then says, "We were at the same funeral. Then over a year later we're in the same room. In entirely different cities, on entirely different coasts. Isn't that weird?"

"Yeah," I say.

"*Yeah,*" Carly mimics, to mock me. Then let's out a *pfft.* "How many movies had you pitched before? Or even written?"

"None," I say.

"Exactly," she says. "So it's fucking weird."

I stop resisting, and nod because she's right.

"Now, can you tell me, who's Sarah?"

"You know," I say.

"No," she says, and reaches out. Before her hand lands on my forearm, I fear it'll feel like fire. "But really."

My neck tightens. I roll my shoulders, but it doesn't help.

"The funeral," I say. "Sarah's."

"Nope!" she says. "That funeral was for Jennifer's suicide. She was a friend of a friend."

Right then, a jolt fires through me, and something unlocks. To hold it in, I picture Sarah's flower-patterned dress.

The wind lifting her hair. Those weeks after, when I barely left the house. When the number of interactions in my day topped out at zero.

"By all accounts," Carly says, "and I mean this in the nicest way possible, there *is* no Sarah."

"That's not true," I object.

"Okay," she relents. "I didn't come here to shake up any delusions."

This time I don't protest.

"You're so fucking weird, man," Carly says, after an exhale. "Or crazy. In fact, let's say crazy because that better explains why, of all the people in the world, I called you. It's the clearest indication that I have terrible taste in men, and no shame."

Carly gestures to the bartender, asking for the bill.

"I'll take care of it," I tell her.

"Fine."

"I know what I have to do next," I say.

"Cool," she says like she's over it. Followed by a head-shaking laugh. "Good luck with your to-do. I'm going to get some sleep. Call me if you're ever not an asshole."

FORTY-NINE

ONCE HOME, I HEAD to my bedroom and open my laptop. While Ryan and Elsa giggle in the living room, I go to Craigslist, then to Missed Connections. I click [**post**]. I type in the only word that can solve all of this. I type in: *Sarah?*

❖❖❖

IN THE MORNING, WHEN I wake, I reach over and check my inbox where I find three new emails. All different responses to *Sarah?*

The first:

I figure, since I'm Sarah, it's best I write and push things forward. So, consider forward pushed.

The second:

lets skip the witty email exchanges and meet soon.

The third:

Finally.

FIFTY

I'M WALKING DOWN HAIGHT Street with the first of the three **Sarah?**s. It's afternoon. Above me, a gray sky zips menacingly by. "Oh," she says, "Poor Travis."

Travis's picture is stapled to a piece of particle board leaned against a wall. Painted at the top of the particle board, in block letters, is "Travis RIP," with no period after the P. On and around the board are handwritten notes from friends, a typewritten poem, and four other small pictures.

Sarah? holds her brown hair clear of her face to get a clearer look. "This poor guy died of an overdose," she says. My eyes blur from a burst of wind. "How awful."

I don't look at the board.

"And this girl was with him," she says, and points. I make like I'm looking, but don't. I look off, and nod.

"What do you say to someone that close to death, y'know?"

I do.

She exhales. "That's some intimate shit."

I open my mouth, but nothing comes out.

"Hey, you okay?" **Sarah?** says to me. "You look way pale."

I feel like pressure's built up all through me, and there's a chokehold around my throat. All I can do is nod.

"Thomas? Do you want me to get help?"

I shake my head, then hunch over, put my hands on my knees to help me relax.

"Should I get help?" she asks.

I shake my head.

"I don't know what to do," she says.

A fist twists inside my chest. "Please go," I gasp. She touches me on the back.

"I can't just leave you."

"Just go!"

❖❖❖

THE SECOND IN THE short line of **Sarah?**s sits across from me at Blowfish Sushi and says, "I'm so sorry that I'm late."

I tell her, "It's fine."

"Though, sometimes when I'm late, and I know this is grim, but I'm like, what if I'm on time and a car hurtles through an intersection and takes me out?"

The waitress appears out of nowhere and asks what we'd like to drink.

"Oh, hi," **Sarah?** says.

We both ask for tap water.

"It's like we can't know whose lives—or deaths, really—we're participating in or denying when we step out the door," **Sarah?** says. "If we're two minutes later, two minutes earlier. If we're on time."

"Are you serious?" I say.

"Uhh, I think so?"

The waiter sets two waters on our table. "You guys ready to order?"

"No," I say, without looking away from **Sarah?**

"Ooookay," the waiter says. "I'll come back in a minute."

"Who put you up to this?" I ask.

"Up to what?" she says.

"*This,*" I say. I can feel myself getting hysterical. Feel that fist in my chest finding its grip.

Sarah? looks around and asks, "Is there a Candid Camera in here, right now? Because I have no idea what you're talking about, and you're super hostile over I don't know what."

I take a deep, centering breath. "Of course you do," I say.

"I believe that's my cue." As she pushes back, her chair noisily rakes the floor. She stands and says, "See ya."

❖❖❖

THE NEXT AFTERNOON I'M at home, readying to leave so I can face off against the third and final installment of **Sarah?** when Ryan comes into my room holding open my Missed Connections notebook. "Dude, what the fuck?" he asks.

"It doesn't matter."

"I think it might," he says, angry, as he hurriedly riffles through a notebook full of dated, scribbled descriptions of women I had no intention of meeting upon first sight. "I logged into your account—I'm the one that set it up, remember? It's loaded with this shit." He holds the notebook and shakes it at me. When I reach for it, he pulls it away. "Have you even *started* the Elvis script?"

"Yeah," I say as I look down at the tops of my shoes.

"Show me."

I stammer when I tell him, "I mean, kind of."

"Kind of!? What the fuck!?"

I want to lean on the excuse of my mother, she's dead. Or Sarah, I think I've finally found her. Instead I turn away.

"Oh, fuck this," he says, and spikes the notebook on the ground. "I've given you all the space and time you could ever need. But you're off wandering the fucking city, jotting down notes about a bunch of nobodies. Christ! I'm a fucking enabler!"

"All the time and space?" I ask, turning back to him. "Netflix knocks, and you're off to Los Angeles with barely a goodbye."

"That's not fucking true."

"And your grand plan is I write it on my own? Like I know what the fuck I'm doing?"

"You said you could."

"*You* said I could."

"Okay," he says. "*Maybe.* So then why lie? Why say you're writing it at all? Why lie to me about your mom? About Sarah? About fucking *everything*!?"

"I don't know."

"Which is okay when you're not fucking it up for everybody else. This project isn't a lark for me, it's my life. This script is due, it's *due,* in three weeks. Or we get paid *shit.* And instead of doing it—for me, or for us, or for your own well-being—you're off doing whatever the fuck with this Missed Connections bullshit. Which, by the way, is *no* kind of answer to *any* problem."

"I was close to realizing that on my own," I tell him, calming. "But now it's being force-figured out for me."

"I have no idea what the fuck that means. Which is a recurring theme, because I have no idea what the fuck anything means with you anymore. I get that you're hurting, but any time I talk to you it's all lies and vague bullshit. Which is *painful.* I don't know what to do, or how to help, or how to be a friend to you in any way. And I can't figure out why you can't be straight with me."

"Is everything okay?" Elsa asks, peeking in, a look on her face that's shot-through with worry.

Ryan and I go quiet. I pick up the notebook and set it on my bed.

"To tell the truth," I say, "it's almost over."

"What is?" Elsa asks Ryan as I brush past her on my way out of my bedroom.

"I have no fucking idea," Ryan tells her, and follows me into the hall.

I open the front door to go.

"You're off the movie, dude," Ryan says, exhausted. "You'll get a few bucks. A 'story by' credit. But we're done."

"Everything okay?" Elsa asks Ryan.

"He hasn't done shit on the script," he tells her. As the door closes behind me, I hear him say, "Let's pack up and go."

❖❖❖

AT A CAFE AROUND the corner from my front door, I'm feeling fragile when the third, and final, **Sarah?** says, "You're not who I thought you were."

"Oh, *really*," I say, unsurprised.

"You're not, no."

"I know your parable," I say. "I figured you out on the walk over."

"My parable?" she asks.

"Well, your *script*, I guess."

"Huh?"

My phone rings, and it's Ryan. I press a button to silence the ring. He calls right back, and I ignore the call. He starts texting, so I turn the phone off.

"You're here to teach me that Sarah isn't my one true collision, because her feelings weren't reciprocal. But what your script doesn't say is she keeps coming back."

Sarah? tilts her head, searching my face for some clue.

I ask her, "Why would she do that if there was no connection?"

Sarah? leans forward and tells me, "If this is some kind of joke, and I'm supposed to know what you're talking about, I don't."

"Oh, that's smart. Let me ramble on so I declare the folly of my behavior. At least tell me I'm getting warmer."

Sarah? says, "To get facts straight, I came here to meet a guy I met two months ago at The Cat Club. He asked for my number, and I declined because he was leaving for Istanbul for six weeks. He said when he was back he'd post only my name on Missed Connections, in case I changed my mind about the phone number. I don't know what's going on with you, but I'm not *your* Sarah. Though I guess I'm willing to be his."

She stands up to go. As she heads to the exit, I tell her, "You can tell Sarah I said, fine, okay, I'm ready."

FIFTY-ONE

A s I STAGGER SLOWLY toward home in darkening
San Francisco night, I get a call from **Blocked ID.**

I answer, but instead of a hello, all I offer is my breathing.

"Ryan reached out to me on Facebook," Sarah says.
"That time in Union Square? I get it now."

"That time in Union Square" was fifteen months ago—
ten weeks before I relocated to San Francisco—when every
rooftop felt like a threat. I'd been sitting alone on a bench in the
smother of Central Park's late-June heat when Sarah walked
by. "Thomas," she said. "What happened to your face?"

"You saw," I said, embarrassed.

My face looked like the mushy remains of a rotting orange,
my eyelids like crushed bees had been smeared on them, from
when The Fucking Man hit and hit me just two weeks before.

"Saw what?" she asked.

My tongue found a healing cut inside my bottom lip where
the skin was ridged and raw. The swelling had dissipated, but if
I opened my mouth too wide there'd be blood.

"Tell me what's going on," she said.

The truths I couldn't tell her: It was my fifth straight
day here; I was forcing myself to leave the house; I knew

she sometimes walked this route on weekdays; I wanted her to see my face, a visual of how much my heart was hurting.

"If I could promise you one meal, what cuisine would be best?" I asked her.

She looked at me confused. "What?"

It was a Tuesday afternoon. I'd been telling my supervisor at the firm that I was at a psychiatrist because of the battered state of my face. I didn't even have a psychiatrist and maybe—Sarah right here, right now—that wasn't the best thing in the world.

"And what's the place you most want to go in the world?" I asked.

Her brow darkened. People with ugly dogs on short chains walked by.

"Next time, I need to get it right."

"Stop it, Thomas," Sarah said.

"Stop it, Thomas," I echoed.

I envied her outfit: denim shorts and a tank top. My jeans were so hot against my legs. I hadn't rolled up the sleeves of my collared shirt.

"Will you just please go see your mother?"

"This is so weird," I said. "I thought you didn't talk since you jumped."

"What are you talking about? What the hell's going on with you?"

Dizzied by Sarah's proximity, I closed my eyes and slumped down low. When I crossed my arms, I felt tinkles of sweat pop up all over my body. After a few seconds, I peeked to gauge her reaction. But Sarah was walking away, wiping her eyes.

Now Sarah asks, "Thomas?" as I approach the front door of my apartment. "You still there?"

I pull out my keys, and their jangling tells her I am.

"I tried to keep going," she says. "But since you weren't willing to go to your mother, I couldn't believe you'd be there when I needed you. In the end, I had no choice but to end it. I loved you, I did, I do still, but you'd built up walls so high."

"Where are you now?" I imagine her as breathable ether, a blend of sparkling light and calming sea mist.

"Austin," she says. "Still in Austin." My throat catches. Sarah takes a deep breath, then in her serious voice tells me, "Thomas, I need you to stop pretending I'm the girl you saw jump."

"I don't know what you're talking about," I say, my hands shaking.

"You do."

"Just meet me on my roof," I say, before I hang up and turn off my phone. "I'll leave the door open."

FIFTY-TWO

IT'S DARK WHEN I enter my apartment. I leave the front door cracked open, and in refracted moonlight, I feel my way to the living room. There I find Ryan's keys on the coffee table, atop a check he's left for the next two months' rent. I scan the room, then look under his cot. His and Elsa's bags are gone.

I head to the back porch and before I'm there I hear the *pat-pat-pat* of feet rising up the back stairs.

I follow, and on the roof, on the far ledge, standing with her back to me, is Sarah. From this distance she's grayed out in the night, a dusty figure with a charcoal waterfall of hazy hair.

I take the replicated moment in. In place of the sun-swept Brooklyn Bridge is the moon-soaked Golden Gate. Instead of a wash of sunlight, the stars are needle pricks in the black velour sky.

I expect some seam in this world to unzip. For the scenery around me to disintegrate for dramatic effect. For invisible dust flecks to bang deafeningly together, or for the circles of my fingerprints to achieve voice.

Then a wind gust riffles Sarah's dress—navy flowers on ghost-white—and I snap to. I step toward her, and don't stop.

"I'll dress appropriately for all occasions," I say, as my feet grumble against the smooth stones that cover the rooftop. "I'll leave notes on your pillow every morning."

When I'm close, she turns, knotted strands of hair covering her face. Her eyes fluorescent pearls. On her arm, in dry-erase marker, she's written, *It was sweet then. But stop.*

"I'm going to get it right this time," I tell her.

You never, ever can.

"Let me save you."

Her shoulders slump and she shakes her head, she's so perturbed. *Like I ever needed saving.*

"Then I'll come with you."

I take a timid step forward. Beyond Sarah, the city is dim lights. The city is damp mist fog. My teeth chatter. I'm close enough to touch her.

Then this: Sarah reaches up with both hands to pull knotted strands of her hair away from her face. When she tucks her hair behind her ears, and looks up, I finally see this someone, this stranger—cheeks blotched red, mouth bent into a frown, Jennifer.

A gulf expands between us.

I teeter backward as she adjusts her feet, delicate, so she can locate the perfect spot. Then she starts to rock, left then right.

There is no slow motion. No stalled moment of wonder.

She looks at me, then she collapses off the ledge.

There, then not there.

I go to the ledge, lean out as far as I can, so I can see into the glint of the misty city. I lift my knees onto it, inch out even farther.

But this woman, this ghost, this never-Sarah, is nowhere.

"Thomas!" a faraway voice shouts. My father's. "What the hell!?"

I'm stunned to see my dad is standing on the street below, a backpack over one shoulder, looking up at me with a frightened expression, mouth agape.

"Fuckhead!" Ryan shouts behind me. Followed by the hurried crunch of running on rooftop gravel.

I don't move. I don't speak.

When the pounding strides get close, I clench my whole body tight and lean my head back away from the ledge. From behind, Ryan grabs me by the shirt back and yanks me down. We tumble down hard onto a cold bed of stones.

"You *ass*hole," he says, and punches me hard in the stomach. I exhale an *oof!* then double-over, trying not to vomit.

"I was just looking."

"Well, stop!" he says and grabs my shirt collar. "Stop this fucking *bullshit.*" There are tears in his eyes.

"Okay," I tell him, and rest my cheek and ear on the gravel.

"Sarah messaged me in a panic and said you'd be up here. You need to get help," he says. "Like really serious help."

"I know," I say. "I will. I swear I will."

Ryan slumps off me, and sits up. His arms resting on his knees. "You're a fucking idiot," he says.

"I know," I say.

I hear the back door open. Elsa's voice. My dad's. Their footsteps on the deck, then their hurried trudge up the stairs.

My father comes toward me, a hobbled run.

"Dammit, Thomas. You scared the hell out of me," he says. When he gets to me, he kneels. His face is streaked with panicked tears. He scoops his arm under me, and lifts, so he's holding me. "Are you okay?"

I nod, but it's another lie. So I correct myself by shaking my head against him. He puts his hand on the back of my head, and draws me toward him, to settle me.

"My son," he says, and brings me closer. "My beautiful boy."

I want to tell him I'll be okay, I just need time, that I'm sorry, I'm sorry. But my throat catches, and all I can offer up is a stifled gasp.

"I know," he says, to quiet me. "I know, I know, I know."

ACKNOWLEDGMENTS

THANK YOU TO ALL the people who said keep going. And yes you can. To all the people who read my work. Or asked to read my work. Who asked me questions and listened.

Thank you to my publisher, Tyson Cornell, for saying yes to this book and making my lifelong dream come true.

To my agent, Farley Chase, who called my writing virtuosic and restored my belief in my fiction.

To my editor, Seth Fischer, who could see what I could not, and whose rigor and relentlessness were essential.

Thank you to Beck's *Sea Change* album, specifically the song "Lost Cause," to which many of the saddest parts of this book were written.

Thank you to Mark Strand and his story "Space," which I read all the way back in 2002.

Thank you to Tobias Wolff, Amanda Filipacchi, George Saunders, Marilynne Robinson, Etgar Keret, Dave Eggers, Aimee Bender, Richard Ford, Ben Fountain, Stephen King, and Chuck Palahniuk.

Thank you to my friends who put up with me and supported this book knowingly or unknowingly: Ben Mainwaring, Matt Herlihy, James J. Williams III, Pierre Blaizeau, Shya Scanlon, Rish Manepalli, Sabrina Howells, John Davison, J. Ryan

Stradal, Amelia Gray, Jacob Tomsky, Dakota Lupo, Kevin Dolgin, Pia Z. Ehrhardt, Roy Kesey, John Leary, and Mike Young. I realize I am forgetting most everyone, including you, and I'm going to be very embarrassed that you are not listed in here, but please do trust when I emphatically apologize and tell you that I should have listed you here. I promise I mean it.

Thank you to my brothers and sisters, my father, and most especially my mother, who lives so strongly in this book and who's roar lives so strongly in me.

And thank you to Morgan Tanswell, whose love and care for this book, and for me, were the rocket fuel needed to bring it, and me, from there to here.